The Magic Door

Unlocking Imagination

Edited By Debbie Killingworth

First published in Great Britain in 2023 by:

Young Writers
Remus House
Coltsfoot Drive
Peterborough
PE2 9BF
Telephone: 01733 890066
Website: www.youngwriters.co.uk

Printed and bound in the UK by BookPrintingUK
Website: www.bookprintinguk.com
YB0539Y

Foreword

Welcome reader, come on in and enter a world of imagination!

This book is jam-packed full of stories on a whole host of topics. The Magic Door was designed as an introduction to creative writing and to promote an enjoyment of reading and writing from an early age.

A simple, fun activity of imagining a door and what might lie on the other side gave even the youngest and most reluctant writers the chance to become interested in literacy, giving them the key to unlock their creativity! Pupils could write a descriptive piece about what lay beyond their door or a complete adventure, allowing older children to let their ideas flow as much as they liked, encouraging the use of imagination and descriptive language.

We live and breathe creativity here at Young Writers – it gives us life! We want to pass our love of the written word onto the next generation and what better way to do that than to celebrate their writing by publishing it in a book!

Each awesome author in this book should be super proud of themselves, and now they've got proof of their imagination and their ideas when they first started creative writing to look back on in years to come!

There is nothing like the imagination of children, and this is reflected in the adventures in this anthology. I hope you'll enjoy reading their first stories as much as we have.

Contents

Arnold Lodge School, Leamington Spa

Abdul Khan (9)	1
Lucy Goddard (10)	2
Harriet Hartog (8)	4
Ehkam Kandola (6)	5
Kasper (10)	6
Teddy Aldersley (10)	7
Harri Shoker (6)	8
Izzy Colledge (10)	9
Luna James (6)	10
Max Barnett-Gagg (5)	11
Grace Rendall (6)	12
Joshua Norman (7)	13
Anaïs Bradley (6)	14
Scarlett Birtwisle (6)	15
Joshua Ariba (6)	16
Alice Bedford (5)	17
Albert Noble (6)	18
Maya Ebrahim (6)	19
Sophia Norman (5)	20
Innes Weir (5)	21
Arthur Hills (5)	22
Henrietta Nunn (5)	23
Emelia Bedford (5)	24
Teddy Hartog (5)	25
Max Hedley (5)	26
Harry Bates (5)	27

Brill CE School, Aylesbury

Emmy Boyle (7)	28
Evie Chanel (7)	29
Toby Southeard (6)	30
Isla Theriault (6)	31

Nellie Stringer (7)	32
Benjamin Poote (7)	33
Jessie Harvey (6)	34
Libby Willis (7)	35
Carys Arnott Winpenny (6)	36
Holly Beckenham (6)	37
Connie Hobbs (7)	38
Lily Ward (6)	39
Zachary Martin (6)	40
Gareth Flasck (7)	41
Dominic Brown (7)	42
Alex Hale (6)	43
Maddie Hope (6)	44
Florence Hill (6)	45
Iris E (7)	46
Samuel Tuffley (6)	47
Georgie Flynn (6)	48
Harper Hemmings (5)	49
Joseph Vincent (6)	50
Woody Shelford (5)	51
Henry Williams (5)	52
Arthur Smith (6)	53
Toby Lambert (5)	54
Oscar Hubbocks (5)	55
Nena Roberts (6)	56
Sonny Murray (6)	57
Annabelle Hawkes-West (6)	58
Orla West (5)	59

Christ The King Catholic Primary School, Bromborough

Isaac Shevlin (9)	60
Joe Delaney (8)	62
Penelope Whittaker (9)	64
Jacob Barker (9)	65

Edith Charles (9)	66
Bridie Mealor (9)	67
Asher Gati (8)	68
Hugo MacMillan (8)	69
Harry McCrary (8)	70
Leo Wu (8)	71
Cora McWha (9)	72
Molly May McGuinness (8)	73
Olivia Hatton (8)	74
Ronan Madden (8)	75
Millie Walker (9)	76
Austin Lucas (8)	77

Crosshall Junior School, Eaton Ford

Alice Hackett (7)	78
Finnley Thompson (9)	80
Scarlett Ascroft-Walker (7)	82
Esele Freeman (9)	83
Kayleigh Bird (11)	84
Corban Lee (9)	85
Maia Wiggett (8)	86
Carmen Salan Borrego (7)	87
Rosalie Hannibal (11)	88
Zoe Crane (8)	89
Harrison Allen (9)	90
Amelia Bumstead (8)	91

Monkwray Junior School, Whitehaven

Keegan Bowman (10)	92
Noah Groggins (8)	94
Dylan McKee (10)	95
Layla Bruce (9)	96
Theo Lofthouse (9)	97
Mya Burns (10)	98
Caleb Fletcher (9)	99
Thomas Holliday (9)	100
Olivia Knowles (9)	101
Savanna McLaughlin (8)	102
Byron Hewer (9)	103
Evelyn Kirkbride (9)	104

Cooper McNally (8)	105
Mia Casson (10)	106
Chloe Davidson (9)	107
Joan Tryphena Ashwin (9)	108
Millie Shaw (9)	109
Jayden Martin-Nicholson (8)	110
Leo Dobson (10)	111
Connor Hodgson (9)	112
Koby Johnston (8)	113

Potten End CE Primary School, Potten End

Iona Taylor (7)	114
Lottie Crouch (6)	115
Abbie Swift (6)	116
Felicity Roberts (7)	117
Spencer South (7)	118
Sophia Farrington (6)	119
Marcus Horner (7)	120
Skyler Alexander (6)	121
Heidi Clark (7)	122
Fleur Taylor (6)	123
Ritchie Chillingworth (7)	124
Charles Coventry (7)	125
Lyla Gwynne (7)	126
Aaliyah Geddes (6)	127
Cassius Horner (7)	128
Sky Wiggan (6)	129
Ava Whiting (7)	130
Phoebe Deaton (6)	131
Vienna-Violet Green (7)	132
Hugo Harrap (6)	133

Waterside Primary School, Hanley

Zeenat Noori	134
Cato Conibear (10)	136
Ianis Papuse (8)	138
Madison Wainwright (8)	140
Sophie Smith (7)	142
Ellia Ratcliffe (7)	144
Jesme Kassai (10)	146

Aisha Qasimi (9)	148	Lucy McCluskey (10)	212
Brianna Chadwick (10)	149	Becca Yeoman (10)	214
Sabahat Amanyar (8)	150	Avah Marshall (10)	216
Lara Bernardes (8)	151	Amber Marshall (10)	218
Aisha Hannah Isa Hafizs (6)	152	Kaitlyn Clark (10)	219
Myles Logan (6)	153	Kearyn Adamson (10)	220
Mikael Mohd Zaid (8)	154	Ibrahim Mohammed (9)	221
Gabriel Gaisie (7)	155	James Halliday (10)	222
Asra Amanyar (6)	156	Phoebe Bees (10)	223
Muneeb Shaikh (7)	157	Ellie Wright (10)	224
Jocelyn Williams (7)	158	Kai Keogh (9)	225
Antonia Cernat (8)	159	Arran Singh (10)	226
Millie Ellis (6)	160	Jamie Moffat (10)	227
Zarnish Imtiaz (6)	161	Arran Campbell (10)	228
Lily Upton (7)	162	Kaleb Watson (10)	229
		Lewis Thomson (9)	230

Woodburn Primary School, Dalkeith

		Harley Dean (10)	231
		Harrison Gifford (10)	232
		Praise Mhango (10)	233
Zia Clarck (10)	163		
Noah McFarlane (10)	164		
Ava McPhee (10)	166		
Joshua Tennant (10)	168		
Adam McKechnie (9)	170		
Amie McGuire (10)	172		
Abbie Rowe (10)	174		
Robbie Hamilton (10)	176		
Ben Barnes (9)	178		
Sophia Goodwin (10)	180		
Erin Casserly (10)	182		
Harris Diamond (10)	184		
Mylie Redpath Hamilton (10)	186		
Isaac Uwagbole (10)	188		
Alexander Wrobel MacPhee (10)	190		
Bethan Clelland (10)	192		
Josh Johnston (10)	194		
Harvey Morland (9)	196		
Amelie McBeth (10)	198		
Ava Costello (10)	200		
Amber Brown (10)	202		
Tolu Oloni (10)	204		
Oliver Lovatt (10)	206		
Lyall Evans-Thomson (10)	208		
Jack Fryatt (10)	210		

The Stories

The Aztec Door

Looking for an adventure, Thor the Viking stumbled upon the mysterious door in the woods. He decided to enter it.

The passage swirled him into a bustling, humid and aromatic future world of the Aztecs. Eyes widening, he saw some tribal leaders devouring brown cubes. Upon finding out it was chocolate (their most prized invention), Thor decided to talk to their emperor, who laid a heavy price.

Exchanging all his gold and silver for chocolate, Thor made his way back through the door. He might have lost all his wealth but he felt like the richest man in the world.

Abdul Khan (9)

Arnold Lodge School, Leamington Spa

The Piger And The Magic Door

Once upon a time, there was a piger. He was half pig and half tiger and he loved the way he looked. The piger lived in Christmas Forest behind the magical door. The door was suspended in mid-air and was covered in glitter. It separated Christmas Forest from the real world. One day, whilst the piger was sleeping, he was suddenly awoken by a loud knock on the magic door. The piger tiptoed to the door and opened it. The door creaked.

Standing behind the door was a donkey and a chicken. The piger said, "Hello, friends," and welcomed them into Christmas Forest.

To the piger's surprise, the donkey and the chicken began to laugh. They said, "Urgh, you look so ugly! What animal are you?"

The piger was shocked and very sad. All the other animals in Christmas Forest had heard the commotion. They said, "If you want to stay this side of the magical door then you must be kind." The donkey and the chicken felt bad and were very sorry.

Their apology was accepted and they all sat together behind the magic door, watching the Christmas lights glisten. The moral of the story is to be kind to everyone.

Lucy Goddard (10)

Arnold Lodge School, Leamington Spa

The Dino Doorway

Sorting Granny's attic started as a dull, dusty job until the boxes in front of me tumbled down to reveal a glowing doorway! The handle shone in the dimly lit attic, inviting me to enter. Once inside I saw palm leaves waving softly in the breeze. On the horizon ash was in the air, shooting from a jagged volcano rising high above the jungle landscape below. I could hear immense thundering footsteps nearby and I slowly turned to see the menacing teeth of a T-rex! Quickly I dashed back to the doorway and the safety of Granny's old attic.

Harriet Hartog (8)
Arnold Lodge School, Leamington Spa

The Magic Land

Once upon a time, I was playing at the park when I found a magic door. I opened the magic door and then it took me to a castle. I opened the castle door and then I saw a witch. I found a horse and I got on the horse. So then I climbed a tree. I found a magic plant and I picked the plant up but I fell. Then I found a letter and it said: 'Go back to the castle' but my horse was going. I searched everywhere and he was nowhere to be seen and then I found a tunnel. I went in the tunnel. I found the horse and then I went back to the castle.

Ehkam Kandola (6)
Arnold Lodge School, Leamington Spa

The Magic Door

It was glowing, it caught my eye. I was turning the handle before I knew it. I cleansed my eyes, but I still saw the same extraordinary features. Strange patterns made of sapphires and emeralds on a door that seemed to be made of pure gold. I had never seen anything like it. I stepped in.

What stood before me was ineffable. An entire world of mysteries. Huge trees with candy cane trunks and candyfloss leaves. A city in the distance that was shaped like a video game console. A road that was a piano. This was a new discovery.

Kasper (10)

Arnold Lodge School, Leamington Spa

Teddy And The Lost Door

Once, there was a boy called Teddy who went to Arnold Lodge School. After school ended he went to a forest five minutes from the school. He went for a walk. By 4:30pm he got to his den made out of wood but when he got there his den was gone. All that was there was a door which was covered with signs and caution tape. Just at that moment, he saw a crack and he looked through it. He saw a sloth on a tree. And out of nowhere, the door opened and he fell through the door. He saw thousands of sloths! A whole jungle to be exact!

Teddy Aldersley (10)
Arnold Lodge School, Leamington Spa

The Magic Trick

Once, in the magic forest, there were some people called Harri, Samuel and Raia and they found a mysterious door. Harri, Samuel and Raia went through and it took them to an exciting candyland! They heard a strange python and so Harry, Samuel and Raia tiptoed past it. "Phew," said Samuel. "That was scary," said Raia.

"Why don't we just carry on exploring?" said Harri. So they carried on and they found a trapdoor and when they opened the trapdoor it took them back home.

Harri Shoker (6)

Arnold Lodge School, Leamington Spa

Wonderland

Once upon a time, there was a girl, her name was Izzy. She once saw a door so she went in and she saw horses and dogs. She rode her favourite horse and her favourite dog. She went onto the path and they were jumping things. If you hadn't guessed Izzy loved jumping over the jumping things with her horse and her dog. The dog always ran around and had lots of fun. So after the jumping she went back and all of the horses were happy because Izzy had a lot of apples for all of them.

Izzy Colledge (10)

Arnold Lodge School, Leamington Spa

Cotton Candy World

One sunny morning I saw some dust and it led me to a magical door. It led me to some magic rainbow world and it was so much fun. But it was time to go. I said to the fairies, "Goodbye," when I was going home. Then I saw a witch. She turned everything grey. Then I saw Anaïs. We fought the witch and then we went home.

Luna James (6)
Arnold Lodge School, Leamington Spa

The Door

I opened the door and went inside and I found some stars and rockets. They were shiny and sparkly. It was so silent. I put on a spacesuit and I found some aliens and I made friends with them. The aliens were green and they were wobbling around. We went on an adventure and saw some meteors.

Max Barnett-Gagg (5)

Arnold Lodge School, Leamington Spa

The Door

When I went through my door I saw a ghost. I felt scared but then I had an idea. I knew ghosts hated oranges so I went to get some. When I got back the ghost ran away. I was happy that the ghost had run away. Then I went back through my door. I found myself in my bedroom safe and sound.

Grace Rendall (6)
Arnold Lodge School, Leamington Spa

The Magic Door

Once upon a time, when I was walking, I saw a door and when I opened the door I went through. I was in a forest. So when I was in the forest I saw a map in the tree and when I opened the map it took me back home. When I arrived home I went to my sitting room and I lived happily at home.

Joshua Norman (7)
Arnold Lodge School, Leamington Spa

The Magic Door

One sunny day I went in the forest and I saw a magic door. I went inside and it led me to the North Pole. It was cold. There was a fairy. It gave me some warm clothes and I saw Santa Claus. I stayed there for a bit. Then it was time to go home and the wind took me home.

Anaïs Bradley (6)
Arnold Lodge School, Leamington Spa

Rainbow Land

One sunny day I found a magic door. I opened the door. I saw a rainbow world. It was beautiful. It was exciting and amazing. I found a fairy. It was nice. Then I had to go back so I opened the door. I went through the door then I went back home.

Scarlett Birtwisle (6)

Arnold Lodge School, Leamington Spa

The Fairy Door

Once upon a time, we saw the magic door. My dad opened the door, then we saw the fairy. The fairy went out of the door. We saw some rainbows. The rainbows were on the wall. The rainbows went away. Then we went back home.

Joshua Ariba (6)
Arnold Lodge School, Leamington Spa

The Door

Once upon a time, I went to Candy Land. When I got there I saw a lollipop. There were rainbow lollipops as tall as giraffes. Then I saw a chocolate lollipop with brown buttons. Then I saw a rainbow in the sky.

Alice Bedford (5)
Arnold Lodge School, Leamington Spa

The Door

I opened the door and I saw Power Rangers. They looked scared. I thought I felt happy and we fought in the forest. We had a battle against the Void Knight and we won. The Void Knight surrendered.

Albert Noble (6)
Arnold Lodge School, Leamington Spa

The Door

I found a magic door. I went through and found a stage. I saw pretty dancers on stage. They were doing amazing dances and at the end they shouted, "Merry Christmas!"

Maya Ebrahim (6)
Arnold Lodge School, Leamington Spa

The Door

When I went to Lollipop Land I saw lollipops and I tasted a lollipop. It was yummy! It was colourful and slippery. They had red and pink ones and also grey ones.

Sophia Norman (5)

Arnold Lodge School, Leamington Spa

The Door

I found the magic door and went through. On the other side, I saw Power Rangers. I asked them if I could have a Power Ranger suit and then I fought beside them.

Innes Weir (5)

Arnold Lodge School, Leamington Spa

The Door

When I went through the magic door I found a gold room. Even the water was golden but the grapes were blue. I played with my puppy called Piglet there.

Arthur Hills (5)
Arnold Lodge School, Leamington Spa

The Door

When I went through the door I found a secret room with lots of presents. I saw lots of elves. I saw Father Christmas, reindeer and lots of presents.

Henrietta Nunn (5)

Arnold Lodge School, Leamington Spa

The Door

When I went through the door I saw a rainbow in the sky. I liked the rainbow, it was really colourful. I climbed the rainbow and used it as a slide.

Emelia Bedford (5)

Arnold Lodge School, Leamington Spa

The Door

I had to climb up a ladder to get to the door. There were really tall ramps. Suddenly I heard roaring motorbikes. They jumped on ramps.

Teddy Hartog (5)

Arnold Lodge School, Leamington Spa

The Door

I went through the door and found a rainbow. It was so colourful and it was bright. It made me very excited. I went to explore.

Max Hedley (5)

Arnold Lodge School, Leamington Spa

The Door

Once upon a time, I went to a place called Rocket Land. There were loads of rockets. They all had rainbow lights.

Harry Bates (5)

Arnold Lodge School, Leamington Spa

Magic Forest

I woke up as the sun was setting one afternoon. I went out to my garden and out of the corner of my eye I saw a glistening door. Hesitantly I stepped towards the strange door. I opened it. I was going to face my fears! I stepped in. There was a swirling mist all around me. I was excited to see what was going to happen. I landed in a rainforest. I heard a hissing sound. A fire-breathing dragon flew towards me. It flew me to an amazing crystal castle where there was a beautiful queen. "Who are you?" I said.

"I have brought you here. I am going to tell you something. Hop on my dragon."

I went on the dragon. "Weee!" We landed at my house. I said, "Bye-bye."

I went back through the door into my bedroom!

Emmy Boyle (7)
Brill CE School, Aylesbury

Winter Wonderland

Once I opened the magic door I smelt the shimmering flowers, they smelt beautiful. From below and out the corner of my eye I saw a door and someone doing a ballet show. She was about to do a curtsey with a pink rabbit and standing right in front of me was a reindeer. I hopped onto it and actually it was Santa's reindeer. He was coming down with his sleigh and he gave me a present. Right behind me was a candy factory. I went inside it and I saw a comfy bed. I lay on it and my eyes drifted into the darkness. I fell asleep. In the morning, when I woke up, I had an Advent calendar on my bed. I opened number one and I got a chocolate. I went out of the factory and back through the magic door. It was quite an adventure!

Evie Chanel (7)
Brill CE School, Aylesbury

The Adventures At The North Pole

On Monday morning my mum let me go outside for 15 minutes but when I opened the door to get outside... it was snowing and there were Christmas trees, elves and even reindeer! It was Santa's workshop!

I saw them loading the presents for Christmas Day into the sleigh. Then I went to say hi to Santa and he let me look at the elves making presents for good children. He even let me ride in his sleigh while he was driving. Then he let me stroke all his reindeer, it was really fun.

But it was only five minutes till I had to stop playing outside so he let me carefully drive his sleigh, it was amazing. Before going back I waved goodbye and went back through the magic door and went back home to relax.

Toby Southeard (6)
Brill CE School, Aylesbury

The Super Happy Magic Forest

One day I was strolling through the woods when my eyes spotted a sparkling door. As I opened it my own two eyes were staring at a magic forest. I glanced at spontaneous unicorns doing acrobatics plus gymnastics. A beautiful fairy, flying very gracefully, was coming in my direction! She said, "I am the fairy snow queen! Come with me!"
The snow queen carefully led me to a group of cute swans! I hesitantly waved. They did the dance of Swan Lake. Some goblins, elves, pixies, pegasuses and horses came and we all had a pool party. It was really late. I opened the door and went back home.

Isla Theriault (6)
Brill CE School, Aylesbury

The Tale Of Magic

One bright sunny morning I got out of bed and looked out the window. My eyes were glued to a glowing thing in an enchanted forest. So I got some of my friends, Connie, Emmy, Annabelle and Alex. I told them the whole story and then we slowly opened the magic door. I said, "It's an enchanted forest!"

Inside there were pink fluffy rabbits flying around. I looked everywhere. I saw rainbow logs. I went through a cave and I saw another door. We opened the door and we were back home. Then it was time to go to sleep.

Nellie Stringer (7)
Brill CE School, Aylesbury

The Dragon Tomb

At midday, I was busy doing my chores when out of the corner of my eye I saw the most graceful door! I carefully stepped closer to the door and rang the large, shiny gold doorbell with all my might. It was so loud it felt like my eardrums were going to blow up!

A few moments later I recovered from the defending sound then I heard a creak and the heavy wooden door opened, I saw a wolf dragon! So I rode it. When I rode it I felt better and the days passed. Then it was time to go home by the wolf dragon.

Benjamin Poote (7)
Brill CE School, Aylesbury

The Candy Cane Fair

One bright sunny morning I got out of bed and out of the corner of my eye a door appeared. Carefully I stepped in. Frilly butterflies started to do amazing things, it was beautiful. I thought for a moment and I noticed it was a candy cane world. I got out and I saw stars with sweeties. I thought it was a fair. I unwrapped the candy canes and I noticed it was time to go so I ran straight back to the door. I just got back in time. When I got back I had a hot chocolate.

Jessie Harvey (6)
Brill CE School, Aylesbury

The Sparkly Door

Once, in a house in a town, I woke up and went to the garden and saw a spontaneously sparkly door. My eyes were drawn to it. I went down there. I scaredly opened the door but somehow my friend was there and I was in a rainforest. I said, "Is the door magic do you think?"

"Yes, why would we be here?"

"I don't know," I said. "Where did you go? Um, where are you?"

She was never seen again.

Libby Willis (7)
Brill CE School, Aylesbury

The Candy World

One sunny morning I was playing in my den house when I saw a door in the corner, it was glowing. I cautiously crept to open the door and I was sucked in!
I found myself in a candy land. I felt the grass, it was cotton candy. I quickly ate some. I saw little presents running towards me. I gracefully danced with them. I heard my dress in the wind and my mummy calling for me to come home. I hesitantly opened the door and went back home.

Carys Arnott Winpenny (6)
Brill CE School, Aylesbury

The Wonderful Forest

One sunny morning, I went to my treehouse. My eyes were drawn to a wonderful door. When I was in the treehouse I saw a blue shiny dragon. I saw it fly into a cave. I went to the cave. I tiptoed into the cave. The blue dragon was very nice, he let me have a ride. He dropped me into a forest. I went from swooshy vines, it was fun. I saw a scary animal. I was so scared I quickly ran back to my home.

Holly Beckenham (6)
Brill CE School, Aylesbury

The Evil Queen

Apple was playing video games and then her mirror started to glow. She could walk through it so she did. The mirror was a prison. The evil queen put Apple in the mirror prison. Apple quickly threw an apple at the mirror and it shattered. "Oh no!" The evil queen was petrifying. Apple had to become her friend and she made Apple lose all of her friends.

Connie Hobbs (7)
Brill CE School, Aylesbury

The Magic Rainforest

One sunny morning I went to my garden and my eyes were drawn to a glowing door. I carefully touched the door and there was a beautiful rainforest with glowing trees and rainbow laces. Suddenly magic came towards me and it turned me into a fairy. I had beautiful blue wings.
The magic disappeared and I went back to the door. I went back home to eat dinner.

Lily Ward (6)
Brill CE School, Aylesbury

The Wicked Door

One sunny morning I went outside and I saw a magic door. I opened the door and I was in Candy Land. I had loads of candy because it was yummy. I got a tummy ache so I stopped eating the candy and I went back through the magic door, back home. Then I did a little bit of playing. I had dinner until it was night-time. The next day the magic door was gone.

Zachary Martin (6)
Brill CE School, Aylesbury

The Magic Door

My magic door took me to a Minecraft land and I saw a girl. She was wearing black armour and a blue helmet. Then I saw a spontaneous villain in the middle of a village then they turned the whole village on fire. Then the girl went to fight the village!

I ran away to a dragon and it flew me to the magic door. I had a rest and finally, I was home.

Gareth Flasck (7)
Brill CE School, Aylesbury

The Magic Door Of Doom

One morning I stepped into my green garden and my eyes were drawn to the door! I gracefully turned the handle and then I ran back to quickly run through the door but then I was in the rotten Land of Doom!

There was a tiny spider quickly scuttling by. I hesitantly waved but it said, "Oi!" It led me to its master. He spoke parseltongue.

Dominic Brown (7)
Brill CE School, Aylesbury

The Magic Door

One sunny morning I looked outside my window and a door shaped like a bee was in a blue bush. It was curious. I was scared, it had come out of nowhere. I got dressed and went downstairs. I went outside, it was hot. I opened the buzzy bee door. Inside were mixed up things. I went on an adventure. On my adventure, I saw a red butterfly.

Alex Hale (6)
Brill CE School, Aylesbury

The Magic Door

Once upon a time, I saw a door in the back of my garden. It led me to Fairyland. I saw Tinker Bell, it was awesome! I was playing with her and then we were watching magical TV, and we ate rainbow food, it tasted amazing. Then it was time for me to go to bed so I went back through the magic door.

Maddie Hope (6)
Brill CE School, Aylesbury

The Magic Door

Once upon a time, I went in my garden and I went through the magic door. When I opened the door I saw a magic castle. I went in the magic castle and I saw a magic fairy. I danced with the fairy and I put my face on the cake and then they took me to my bed. Then they took me back to my house.

Florence Hill (6)

Brill CE School, Aylesbury

The Dog Land

I came across the most magical door and I carefully opened the magic door. There was a dog. It began to get littler and littler and then there was a humongous dog clambering to watch me and I saw little puppies. After that it was time to go. I waved goodbye and walked back through the door.

Iris E (7)
Brill CE School, Aylesbury

The Magic Door

I woke up in the middle of the night and went into the garden and I saw a magic door. I was scared but I was brave. I crept in and saw a candy pie. I was full of shock. On my way, I saw some ice cream but I was full so I took some home with me.

Samuel Tuffley (6)
Brill CE School, Aylesbury

The Magic Door

One day I saw a magic door in my house. I stepped into the magic door and I was at Disneyland. I could smell hot dogs, I could feel the crackly bottles. I played and never went back. I miss my family but I still like this place.

Georgie Flynn (6)
Brill CE School, Aylesbury

The Magical Door

Once upon a time, in my garden, I saw a magical door. Suddenly I found a fairy land. It was beautiful. I went flying with the fairies. Then I saw the magical door and it took me back to my house.

Harper Hemmings (5)
Brill CE School, Aylesbury

 YoungWriters® Est. 1991

The Football Story

One day I was in my garden and I saw a red door. Then I went through the red door and it took me to a football stadium. I scored and it was noisy. Finally, I jumped back through the door.

Joseph Vincent (6)
Brill CE School, Aylesbury

Spidey's Comin' To Town

There I was. At the back of my garden. I found a lovely door. Suddenly I looked at my hands. I was Spidey! I love Spider-Man!
Soon I saved lots of people till noon. I loved it!

Woody Shelford (5)

Brill CE School, Aylesbury

The Magic Door

One day I found a door in my garden, it was a magic door. I played all day and all night and the next afternoon I saw a giant strawberry. I stayed in the door forever and ever.

Henry Williams (5)
Brill CE School, Aylesbury

The Magic Door

Once upon a time, there was a magic door in my garden. Suddenly I was in a rainforest. There were a lot of snakes. I went climbing with the snakes. I stayed there forever.

Arthur Smith (6)
Brill CE School, Aylesbury

The Story Of The Sandy Beach

One day I went outside and I saw a magic door. Suddenly I sank into the sand. I saw coconuts. Then I found the door. I went through and lived happily ever after.

Toby Lambert (5)
Brill CE School, Aylesbury

Door To Lava Island

Once upon a time, there was a boy. He found a door in the middle of nowhere and he opened the door. It took him to a lava island and he found a lava yeti.

Oscar Hubbocks (5)
Brill CE School, Aylesbury

Through The Magic Door

One day I found a magic door. I opened the door and there was Disneyland.
I hugged and played with Minnie Mouse then I went back through the door.

Nena Roberts (6)

Brill CE School, Aylesbury

The Magic Door

One day I found a door in the playground and it took me to the World Cup. Later I went back through the door and I lived happily ever after.

Sonny Murray (6)
Brill CE School, Aylesbury

The Magic Door

I came across a magic door and I opened the door. I carefully walked through and saw a colourful beach. Next I walked home.

Annabelle Hawkes-West (6)

Brill CE School, Aylesbury

The Magic Door

Once upon a time, there was a little magic door. I went through it and it was snowing. I fell over. It was a snowstorm.

Orla West (5)

Brill CE School, Aylesbury

The Battle Of Star Wars

One day I went up to my attic and saw something with a blanket on. I pulled down the blanket and saw a door with a weird pattern on it. The pattern had a black background with red criss-crossed stripes. I wondered, *do I go in? Yes*, I thought, so I put my hand on the handle, opened it and stepped in.

A long time ago, in a galaxy far, far away, was a boy who didn't know he was a Jedi! I popped out of a toilet and noticed it was the hidden door.

"Oh no!" I screeched, but as I climbed out the toilet I noticed my clothes had mysteriously changed. I was wearing the clothes the Jedi wear, light brown robes and dark brown boots.

I went out of the bathroom and saw people fighting in the corridor of a massive spaceship. I was scared but when I reached into my robes I found something. It was a lightsaber! I turned it on and a bright beam of green light appeared. It was so bright, it looked like a glow stick and I felt like my eyes exploded.

I joined in the battle and saw the stormtroopers trying to capture a man but I stopped them. I felt fine until Darth Vader came and wanted to challenge me. I took the challenge and I defeated Darth Vader by chopping his helmet off. He cried like a baby, so his stormtroopers were going to take him to nursery, but before I saw them do that I ran to the toilet and flushed myself down to go home!

Isaac Shevlin (9)

Christ The King Catholic Primary School, Bromborough

The Attic Of Dreams And Enemies

I was walking around my grandparents' house then I asked, "Can I go up to the attic to get the old action figures?"

My grandad said, "Go on then, Bob, be careful though."

I went up and then I looked for the box. It wasn't there but then I saw a door... I turned the handle. *Whoosh!* I got sucked in but I jumped back out and saw it said: 'Dimension of Raja'. Then I realised I should walk through. I spawned in a castle. I was apparently the king of Raja so I said, "What's good about this place?"

"Well, sir, if you ask you shall receive."

"C-can I have a sweet land and a 700ft Christmas tree?"

"Yeah, sure."

"Sweet!"

I went to Sweetland and got the news. We were under attack from another dimension. I said, "Fine, I'm gonna ask for them to go away."

"You can't do that!"

"Okay, I'll fight... They're gone!"
"What?"
"They all needed the lavatory," I sighed.
"Oh!"
Then I went back to my grandparents' attic.

Joe Delaney (8)
Christ The King Catholic Primary School, Bromborough

The Secret Arcade

Once, there was a young, sweet little girl called Amy. She loved to go to the cool, fun arcade that was local to her house. So on a sunny, bright day on the weekend, she, her mum and her older sister decided to go to the park and get some ice cream and go to the arcade.

When they arrived from the park she ran to her favourite game, Super Mario Bros. The character she loved the most was Princess Peach. Suddenly she noticed a new game was released so she bounced from that game to another and, *bash! Crash! Thud!* She landed in the game station where there was Wreck-It Ralph and Penelope said, "Excuse me, hello. I feel so blessed to be here."

"I know," Ralph said, "Well, you better get going," he said calmly. He gave her a large bear hug.

"Bye," Amy squealed.

The next stop she went to was game school and lots of mini Mario people were there. She learnt lots of game facts. The last stop was Princess Peach's castle and Peach wasn't locked away. She got to see Peach and took loads of photos. After, she found a magic door that took her home.

Penelope Whittaker (9)

Christ The King Catholic Primary School, Bromborough

The Rise Of A Jedi

A long time ago, in a galaxy not so far away... I crept up to a lava door, hoping not to get sunburned. I opened the glowing, red door carefully. The heat was burning my hand and hot air flew at me. I looked down and I was wearing robes.

An old man, who was standing near a white modern building, shouted across the black, volcanic sand, "I've been waiting for you for thousands of years!"

I replied, "I don't even know where I am!"

I looked for my phone to call my mum but in my pocket, I found a shiny, metal stick. There was a button on it. I pressed it and a shiny, glowing beam popped out- *vroom!* I swooped it around like it was a magic wand, not really knowing what I was doing.

The man stepped forward from the shadows and said, "That's a lightsaber. I thought you would have known what it was. It is very rare, do not mess with it. Not many have been discovered. Come with me, I will show you the ways of the force."

Jacob Barker (9)

Christ The King Catholic Primary School, Bromborough

Christmas Jungle

This morning I let my dog out for a morning walk but I saw something so I went to look. I had so many vines around my garden. The only weird thing was that there were vines that I had never seen before and they were ever so close together. There was also a handle so I pushed down. The door opened and I was spinning so fast it was crazy! After I stopped spinning I was a bit dizzy but it looked very Christmassy. I then soon saw a palace. I hoped there was food because I was very hungry.

When I got in there was food and little animals sitting on a big man's lap and that was Santa. He saw me and snapped his fingers and I was on a sleigh and there was a very loud snap. After that, I saw Scrooge and as normal he was grumpy. There was one more loud snap and I was back with my dog and my dad called Terence.

Edith Charles (9)
Christ The King Catholic Primary School, Bromborough

Going Into Space

One day, I was going to bed when suddenly I saw a door. I slowly opened the door and it was so magical. There was the most colourful planet I had ever seen. There were fluffy pink clouds around it and I loved it so much. Pink, purple and blue are my favourite colours. This was the most magical day of my life! I saw an astronaut there and we made friends. We held hands and looked up at the sky and saw the twinkling stars. They looked really close to me. Since I was in space I guess you see everything close to you. We jumped up to the moon, it wasn't that big of a jump. This was a dream come true. I said bye to my new friend and I went back home and back to sleep.

Bridie Mealor (9)

Christ The King Catholic Primary School, Bromborough

Paradise Of Love And Heaven

One day, I was playing in my ordinary garden. I was throwing the ball with my dog and all of a sudden, it went into a bush. The dog ran into the bush. I followed him into the bush. "Argh! Argh!" I was floating and floating until I got to Heaven. I saw my grandma. I held her hand. I went back into the portal to a different dimension. It was a world of love and care where everyone I saw was being nice. I looked down and it was just clouds, it felt like cotton candy.

"It's time to go home," said Grandma.

"No, I want to stay with you," I said.

I said bye and went home and went to sleep.

Asher Gati (8)

Christ The King Catholic Primary School, Bromborough

Temple Of Doom

Once, I was in hot, sunny Las Vegas. I opened my door but when I looked there was a creepy, mysterious temple. I could hear screaming and yelping. Immediately I decided to go in. But when I went in someone grabbed me and took me down into a tomb. He told me I had to get rocks but I didn't. There were loads of children there. I cut my chain off but then, *oh no*, I thought, *a guard is coming.*

One child pulled me down.

"Thank you."

"Anytime!"

I ran for my life out of the temple and went back through the door and I called it the Temple of Doom.

Hugo MacMillan (8)

Christ The King Catholic Primary School, Bromborough

One Day In The Jungle

One day I was going on a trip and I saw a magic door. I opened it and it led me to a jungle. I saw a massive panda and some tigers. The door closed. I got in. I was in shock. It was amazing. I wanted to run around but somebody was home, this was terrible for me. He was coming down. He looked like one of those henchmen so I ran to hide. He spotted me. He said, "What are you doing in my place?"

"Nothing," I said.

He said, "Come out."

I came out. I got attacked by him. I saw a sword to my left. I got the sword and hit him. He fell to the ground.

Harry McCrary (8)

Christ The King Catholic Primary School, Bromborough

Pokémon World

I went to a magic door and when I opened the door there was a gust of fire shooting out. It was Charmander and then I recognise this place, it is a Pokémon world. Suddenly Squirtle attacked Charmander. I watched the battle and all of the sudden Charmander turned into Charmeleon. I continued to watch the battle and finally Squirtle was defeated. I waved goodbye to the next evolution of Charizard, the strongest and the most strong fighter of all the fire type Pokémon. I hoped next time I can go there again. It was so exciting!

Leo Wu (8)

Christ The King Catholic Primary School, Bromborough

Christmas Wonderland

One day, there was a rainbow door. It was glowing so I could not resist but go through it. When I stepped in I felt a fluffy cloud on my feet. I thought that I was in a wonderland. Little did I know I was right so I went to explore. There were Christmas lights everywhere. I kept on walking and in front of me was Santa. Santa showed me his house but it was no ordinary house, it was a treehouse wrapped in lights and was painted red. Then Santa said, "Goodbye," and I gave him the biggest hug ever and then it snowed.

Cora McWha (9)

Christ The King Catholic Primary School, Bromborough

The Christmas Wonderland

One long day I was playing in my garden when I saw a strange-looking door out of the corner of my eye. I slowly walked over and just out of nowhere it opened and nearly hit me in the face. I saw this white stuff all over the trees and then I realised it was snow, silly me! I walked closer and even closer... "Argh!" Sorry that was my reaction when an elf popped out at me and I saw Santa, elves, snowmen and even reindeer. Then I realised it was a Christmas wonderland in my own garden.

Molly May McGuinness (8)

Christ The King Catholic Primary School, Bromborough

Christmas Adventure

One day I was walking outside in my garden when I saw a wardrobe in the middle so I went in it and I saw elves. I heard bells and then while I was walking I saw Rudolph, Santa and more elves. I haven't been more excited in my life! I saw Santa go off on his sleigh. Then I saw snow raining down on me. I saw people in the snow then I joined them. I was so shocked. I saw Santa again then I saw people on the sleigh. I was so excited so then I joined them to deliver all the gifts.

Olivia Hatton (8)

Christ The King Catholic Primary School, Bromborough

Magical Sky

One day I woke up, got dressed and had breakfast then I went out and saw a tree. I started to climb it but then I saw a doorknob so I opened it and I was in the clouds. In the distance, I could see a castle. I heard a stamp, stamp! I was curious so I walked over and I went into the castle and saw a person nearly get executed by the giant. But then as soon as he went to chop off his head I shouted, "Stop! Stop all of this nonsense right now!"

Ronan Madden (8)

Christ The King Catholic Primary School, Bromborough

The Water World

One sweet, sunny day, I had no idea what was about to happen to me. I went to the seaside but I didn't go normally, I went through a secret door at my new home.

It was beautiful, there were fish singing like rock stars on their guitars and crabs dancing like they were from Dance Moms. The craziest thing was I turned into a beautiful mermaid with a rainbow tail and I danced and sang my heart out but then it was time to go home.

Millie Walker (9)

Christ The King Catholic Primary School, Bromborough

Under The Sea

One day I went swimming in the sea. I saw a glowing light. I swam closer. I saw a door. Coral grew around it. I struggled but I opened it. I got sucked in. I appeared in a magical cave, there were mermaids dancing and crabs singing. I joined in and had a good laugh but I had to go back home so I swam back. I said, "Bye," to all my new friends.

Austin Lucas (8)

Christ The King Catholic Primary School, Bromborough

The North Pole

Once upon a time, there lived two children called Tom and Esther. They lived at 11 Snowy Lane, in a very big mansion. One day, Tom was in Esther's ginormous bedroom when... he saw a button with a tiny door. Tom knelt down and pressed the button and he shrank. He pressed the button again and Tom grew back to his normal size. Tom ran to Esther and told her about the small door with the button next to it. "Where?" shouted Esther excitedly.

"Come with me," replied Tom happily.

"This is going to be fun," said Esther.

When they both reached Esther's bedroom, they pressed the button and shrank to elf-sized humans. "Wow!" they said.

They walked through the tiny door that was now the size of them into a magical land of snow and ice. They were speechless. In the distance, they saw a workshop. They ran over to it. When they finally got there they saw a jolly old man wearing red. "I-i-is that S-S-anta?" spluttered Tom.

"Ho ho ho, yes it is!" said Santa happily. "I'm glad you're here Tom, we need help, one of the elves is off sick."

"Wow!" whispered Tom.

"And Esther, I could give you a tour of the workshop!"

"Yay!" screamed Esther with excitement.

Santa told Tom where to sit and make toys and then showed Esther the workshop. The next day, Santa flew them back to the door. They hugged Santa goodbye and walked through the door... But the door stayed there; ready for the next adventure.

Alice Hackett (7)

Crosshall Junior School, Eaton Ford

Cloud World

Some say magic doesn't exist, but it does. I found a magic door while exploring in the Weeping Willow Woods. I looked at the door, it looked peculiar. It looked like it was a cloudy door and it was very misty. I opened it. "Wow! There are so many clouds, so many cloud people and even a cloud castle!"

I walked in it and I could hardly breathe 'cause it was so amazing. On the strange door, there was a hatch with a face peeking through and it said, "What would you like, my fine sir?"

"I really want to explore," I said.

"As you wish."

I just saw some sort of cloud guardian. The guardian was made of clouds, in fact, everything except that door person was made of clouds. Suddenly, I saw a big guard in front of me, he said, "You are trespassing!"

I said, "No I'm not, a weird door person let me i-" I was cut off by a door slamming.

"It's a trap!" said the door person.

I made a run for it out the back door, but I found myself falling down. I saw the cloud castle above me. I found myself stuck in a tree but I fell down.

"Aww!" I exclaimed. "My leg really hurts, but I'll be fine. All I know is I'll never ever go through cloud doors again," I murmured to myself.

Finnley Thompson (9)
Crosshall Junior School, Eaton Ford

The Magic Door

It was a stormy night. Three children called Mia, Jade and Ella were about to go to bed. The next day, Jade went to go and see Mia and Ella in their usual spot. She was worried she'd be late (she normally was) but Mia and Ella weren't there. Instead, there was a big sparkly door. Jade walked very slowly through the door. It led her to a dark, cold night. She could see mostly black but some sparkling stars. Jade could also see a telescope and just as she looked through it she felt something was watching her. But as soon as she took her eye from it she couldn't see what it was but she knew she didn't like the place at all. She felt brave enough to carry on walking. "Ouch!" Jane said as she heard a big bump, it was a treasure chest. "Ouch!" Jane said again. But it wouldn't open. Jane returned with the treasure and there were Mia and Ella. The treasure chest opened and there was loads of treasure for them all.

Scarlett Ascroft-Walker (7)

Crosshall Junior School, Eaton Ford

The French Adventure

Once upon a time, my family and I moved home and that's when I discovered a magic door. I was surprised at first but I saw an earring like a heart and it fit in the shape on the door. I put it in then... *whoosh!* It took me to beautiful Paris in France and I was dressed like a French person. I saw La Tour Eiffel (or just Eiffel Tower). Then I saw a suspicious homme (means man in French). He looked like the man in the poster on the wall which said: 'Person who finds this man will get 200 Euros'.

I saw that man and chased him and he ran but I caught him anyway. People cheered for me and I got the money. My earring glowed and the magic door came. I said, "Bye-bye," and went in. My mum and dad called to ask what the noise was all about and I said, "Nothing!"

I put the money in my huge French piggy bank. That was my first and best adventure. Who knows what adventures await me in the future?

Esele Freeman (9)
Crosshall Junior School, Eaton Ford

The Magic Door

One morning, an 11-year-old girl called Mia woke up to a bright dazzling rainbow flowing through the sky straight to her bedroom door. Mia was puzzled and curious so opened the door. Instead of the normal hallway, she saw a beautiful, enchanted wood. Her senses were full of delight, she could hear the cheerful chirp of the fire and ice phoenixes in the air and the unicorns' hooves swooshing as they pranced around on the grass. Mia could see magical mermaids swimming in a shining, turquoise river. Her nose was overpowered by a delicious fruity smell of gummy sweets. The grin on Mia's face stretched right from cheek to cheek as she felt her heart race with excitement and joy. Without a thought or worry in the world she tiptoed into the fabulous, possibly forbidden enchanted forest...

Kayleigh Bird (11)
Crosshall Junior School, Eaton Ford

Corb's Day At School

One day there was a boy called Corb. He was doing his home learning and he had one problem! He couldn't work out 12 x 12... "Hmm," Corb said. "Wait, I know it. The answer is..."

"Corb, it's time for school!" said his mum.

He ran to school. Finally, he got there and his teacher said, "We are going to see a rocket landing down on the field."

He went onto the field. Suddenly the rocket came down... *Whoosh!*

The rocket came down and a man came out.

"Argh, there are c-creatures!" wailed the man and ran away. While everyone was looking at the man Corb quickly ran into the spaceship. He knocked a red button. "Oh no!" he said. *Whoosh!* He went up in the air.

Corban Lee (9)

Crosshall Junior School, Eaton Ford

Fantasy Land

When I was playing in the soft play area, a magic door appeared. I looked at the blue, magic, sparkly door and said to myself, "I am going to explore behind this door."

I opened the door and I discovered a fantasy land! I was shocked by what I saw. I could see a massive Lego shop with Star Wars in the front window. Next to the horse riding was the invisible restaurant, only visible to me, that had lots of yummy food and fizzy drinks. As I was walking around, I could hear people laughing loudly, because they were having fun. I ran over to the stables to find some horses training for a race. I could hear their hooves trotting. I felt excited for the race. After the race had finished, I ran quickly back to the door to go and tell my family.

Maia Wiggett (8)

Crosshall Junior School, Eaton Ford

The Magic Door Of Christmas

It was one windy and sunny day in summer. I was reading in my bedroom when I heard a noise in the attic. I carefully climbed up the stairs and suddenly I saw an extraordinary door appear out of nowhere.

I decided to do the bravest thing and open that door. The door was magic because I entered a special roller-coaster park at Christmas time. The place was full of children because parents were not allowed.

The park was full of food, toys and sweeties, all free. The children were screaming and laughing on the roller coaster and the smell was like candyfloss.

I had a perfect day until I closed the magic door.

Carmen Salan Borrego (7)
Crosshall Junior School, Eaton Ford

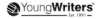

The Enchanted Door

As Amari was taking a stroll on the Hawaiian beach, he saw something in a distant palm tree. "A door!" he exclaimed.

As he entered the impenetrable door, a new biome burst open and it appeared to be snowing.

Just before he took a step outside onto the bleached, glistening grounds, Amari took a glance behind him. Two completely different places stood right next to each other.

It was Sweden. The verdant Northern Lights illuminated the obsidian foggy sky as the dramatic landscape transformed from rolling hills into mountains. Its abundant forests and lakes gleamed on the horizon.

Rosalie Hannibal (11)

Crosshall Junior School, Eaton Ford

The Crazy Journey To Candyworld

One day a girl named Millie was playing tag then she went to have lunch. Then the door glowed multicoloured. She opened the door and she was teleported.

She opened her beautiful blue eyes then she was in a strange land full of amazing candy but then she heard screaming. The people warned her not to go in the dark area but she didn't do what she was told. She walked straight in but then she turned back and ran straight to the door and it opened. She said goodbye and then went home.

Zoe Crane (8)
Crosshall Junior School, Eaton Ford

Arthur's Magic Door Adventure

Once upon a time, there was a boy named Arthur and he was walking his dog on the beach. All of a sudden, he saw a random door. He opened it and saw a forest. Then he decided to go through it and then the door shut. All he saw were trees then he panicked and started to walk and then he saw a tiger. He ran but the tiger saw him and ran to him then Arthur saw another door and went through it. It took him back to the beach. He walked his dog back home and lived happily ever after.

Harrison Allen (9)
Crosshall Junior School, Eaton Ford

The Magical Door

Once upon a time, there was a magical door with magical things inside it. And guess what was in it... There was gold and money and last but not least, games. Everything I stepped on and touched was money, gold and games and of course, I could also see the Arsenal team. My favourite players are Saka and Gabriel Jesus and they gave me more money!

Amelia Bumstead (8)
Crosshall Junior School, Eaton Ford

The Distorted World That Never Ends

Countless moons ago, an infection called 'the eye' (that spreads like cancer) infected the world again but it never infected the children. Leon was wandering the Tower streets, repeating the phrase, "I swear I've been here before..."

"Argh...!" He went to investigate the noise and he came upon a child wearing a yellow overcoat. They both stared at each other as if they had seen each other ten times before. The person screamed. A hulking infected creature stared into their eyes but it wasn't hostile, it panted at them, croaking, "Host, host, you host!"

In that moment, Leon remembered it was the eye's right-hand man. He was the leader of the Tower but he ran and screamed, "I wish the cycle never happened!" And like that, a door appeared. He entered obviously and he saw what would happen. The universe would collapse and everyone would die and everything would be destroyed.

He exited the door and his future self appeared before him. He made him perish so he could continue the cycle forever until the cycle happened again and surely he turned into his future self and... Leon wandered the Tower streets...

Keegan Bowman (10)
Monkwray Junior School, Whitehaven

The Golden Gloves

Once upon a time, there was a boy named George. One night as George slept he heard a noise that woke him up. At first, George was scared but then he saw a bright light coming from under his bedroom door. George opened the door to a voice calling to him. The voice said, "George, we need you."

This made George feel strange but he was excited to explore and he walked into the light. When George came out of the light, he was at the World Cup final with England in a penalty shoot-out against Brazil. England had lost their goalkeeper and asked George to step up.

Amazing for George he couldn't believe where he was but he did not have any gloves. It was then, at this point, he looked down at his hands and he was wearing the golden gloves. George stepped into the goal and saved the final penalty. The crowd's noise vibrated through the pitch, as England won the World Cup with George lifting the trophy, the rest was a blur. George woke up, thinking it was all a dream until he tripped over the golden gloves. The dream was real!

Noah Groggins (8)
Monkwray Junior School, Whitehaven

Jake And The Door

In the middle of a summer's day, Jake was on a school trip when he got off track from his class. In the corner of a room, Jake spotted a dark oak door. Without hesitation, Jake sprinted over to the door and questioned himself, "Why is this here?" Suddenly a light flashed through the door's cracks. Just seeing through his eyes, Jake grabbed the doorknob and twisted it. Jake walked inside and felt the long, green grass beneath his feet. Jake heard colourful birds singing calm songs. Jake walked on and on through the forest, seeing things he'd never seen before. He saw tall, vast oak trees the size of mountains, and a lagoon with clear blue water that had fish of all colours. Without realising it, Jake forgot about his class. As fast as lightning can strike, Jake sprinted back through the vast oak door. Gasping for air, Jake pulled open the door and ran back through the building. Seeing them about to leave, Jake ran, pushing past people. "Wait!" Jake shouted. Jake got to them just in time for leaving.

Dylan McKee (10)

Monkwray Junior School, Whitehaven

The Two Girls - A Fairy Adventure

Once, two little girls were at the park. They were called Crystal and Melody. As they were doing their tricks, a magic door appeared. Crystal exclaimed, "Hey, look, a magic door!"
Melody nervously whispered, "Should we go in?"
Crystal nodded enthusiastically. They went in...
They woke up on a feather bed with fairies surrounding them. Crystal asked, "Hey, should we explore?"
Melody yelled, "Yeah!"
They walked and walked then they saw a large amber creature with four arms coming to destroy the girls. They yelped but had a plan... Crystal got a weapon as Melody was crouched behind the creature. Crystal hit the creature and it tumbled over Melody and disappeared.
They transported back to the park again so they played fairies. They dug up sand and found treasure. It was a fairy pearl. Now they could visit every day.

Layla Bruce (9)
Monkwray Junior School, Whitehaven

Theo, Charlie And The Mysterious Door

One day, there was a boy called Theo and a girl called Charlie. Theo and Charlie were brother and sister. They both loved to go on walks around the beach. They loved going around the beach because there were rockpools that they splashed each other with.

One day, Theo and Charlie were going on a walk when they noticed a door. They walked up to the door and when they got closer they noticed light coming out. They also noticed there were noises coming out. Theo said, "It sounds like a cow and a donkey."

They both opened it and they saw a cow that said, "Miaow!" and a wonky donkey.

"It looks like a galaxy in here," said Charlie.

Theo, Charlie and the animals all went to explore further in the cave. When they reached the end of the cave they realised that it was a normal cave that just had a door to get in.

Theo Lofthouse (9)

Monkwray Junior School, Whitehaven

The Land Of Mysteries

One late, scary night, a little girl called Charlotte got woken up by a luminous light. While stepping out of bed, she mumbled, "Whoa!"

All of a sudden, Charlotte heard a girl whispering, "Come in, don't be scared!"

Opening the door, she gasped. She slowly crept into the room. With a mouth as big as an orange she found a house. She said, "How could there be a house inside a house?"

While trying to find her way to the door, someone tapped her on the shoulder. She looked back and no one was there... She crept out and found her way and ran in. "Hello, is anyone here?" shouted Charlotte.

Suddenly someone yelled, "Leave now!" A big, tall figure chased her.

Finding her way back home she opened the dark brown door and out of breath she said, "I am never going there again!"

Mya Burns (10)
Monkwray Junior School, Whitehaven

A Boy In Santa's Land

One snowy Christmas Eve, a boy called Jake thought, *what would it be like if I went in Santa's workshop?* He was in his pyjamas and he needed to get dressed so quietly, he went to his wardrobe. Opening up the wardrobe he saw something different. It was a blazing light that shone in his eyes and the force of it was sucking him in.

He desperately tried to run away but he was tired and could not. Waking up, he saw little red figures surrounding him. Feeling strange but excited he got up. He realised they were tiny elves and they were leading him to a tall, broad man. Santa Claus! Rushing up the stairs he shook Santa's hand.

"Where are you from?" Santa said.

When Jake was about to explain, he said, "Take this." He handed Jake a small present to take home.

Caleb Fletcher (9)
Monkwray Junior School, Whitehaven

Christmas Magic

One day a boy called Olly uncovered an old brown door that dated back to 1834 (this door was yet to be discovered). The young boy had a peep through...

Olly was instantly sucked in by a strong current, probably the strongest thing ever. Whilst he was flying through, he instantly came to a halt and saw a village of families. Through the shadows of the curtains, he saw singing and dancing to Christmas songs. Olly wished he could stay there longer because there were no electronics, and everyone was a family and spent time together. Olly knew if he didn't get back before the streetlights went off, Santa would bring him coal.

Olly turned round, waved goodbye and walked through the door. He realised that life isn't all about electronics. It's about spending time with family.

Thomas Holliday (9)

Monkwray Junior School, Whitehaven

The Night Before Christmas It's The FIFA World Cup

One early morning, a girl named Charlie had a walk around her estate on Christmas Eve and saw a mysterious door that had never been there before. Then, Charlie opened the door that was there but then she asked herself in her head, *should I walk in?* She said to herself, *yes, I should!* Just then, she walked in and saw the FIFA World Cup (England vs Iran). As fast as lightning, Charlie saw she was on the sidelines of the pitch. She went to the England manager and asked, "How did I get through that mystery door to here?"

The England manager said, "That is a magic door from your estate to here!"

As quick as a flash, Charlie got emotional and at the end of the game, she got an autograph from Kane and Stones.

Olivia Knowles (9)

Monkwray Junior School, Whitehaven

The Girl Who Had No Animal Friends

One morning there was a girl, her name was Masy. She was wearing a neon pink dress and black tights. This girl had friends but she wanted friends that were animals. So Masy set off to find a bunny hole. After some time of searching, she came across a magical door. When Masy stepped through, she was in some type of rainforest. When she got there Masy found a sloth. The sloth said, "Cross this obstacle and I will be your friend. If you don't I'm your enemy!"
So the girl said, "Okay."
Eventually, after passing lasers and jumping logs, the girl made it across so the sloth who said, "I will be your friend."
Masy lived well with her sloth. It was funny and it liked to jump around.

Savanna McLaughlin (8)
Monkwray Junior School, Whitehaven

A Snowy Village

One snowy morning, Kai (a 12-year-old boy) was walking down Weird Street. Kai came upon a door. Full of curiosity, Kai opened the door. There was a smaller door. Kai pushed it open and there was another. There was a village with a sign saying: *Santa Village This Way*.

After a few minutes, he was there. "Ho ho ho, merry early Christmas!" said Santa.

Kai started to run around the village. Santa said, "You are welcome to come and eat with us."

So off Kai went to have tea. Kai, who was happy, ate all his dinner of turkey and stuffing. For dessert was Christmas cake. "Yum yum," said Kai. Sadly Kai said his goodbyes. Kai didn't want to leave Santa's village.

Byron Hewer (9)
Monkwray Junior School, Whitehaven

The Adventure To The North Pole

Once, there lived a girl called Lola, and on Christmas Eve she heard a noise coming from the tree so she went to look. Eventually she found what it was, it was a small button on a table. After thinking, she finally pushed it and she teleported into a winter wonderland. Lola also turned into an elf and Santa appeared so Lola said, "Can you help me find my home?"

Santa said, "Only if you find my hat!"

"Okay," Lola said.

After hours of searching, she found it on a tree and she saw a bird and said to it, "Please can you get the hat?"

The bird said, "Okay."

Once she found Santa she gave it to him. Finally, she got home in time for Christmas.

Evelyn Kirkbride (9)
Monkwray Junior School, Whitehaven

Visiting The World Cup

One morning, a kid aged nine called Harry walked down the street with his father. When he got down really far he saw a shop called Imagination City and he begged his dad to go in and he did. When Harry got in he saw loads of doors and people just disappeared through them and he got so excited. But he saw that to go through it cost £50 so he had to sneak into one and he did that.

He got inside and it was an England vs Brazil game. The World Cup final. He heard the Brazil and England fans cheering on their countries but then there it was, he saw the World Cup trophy. He snuck around the fans, grabbed the trophy and ran through the door again quickly and hugged his dad.

Cooper McNally (8)
Monkwray Junior School, Whitehaven

The Entrance To Valhalla

Once, in Denmark, there was a Viking called Vallhalla (aged 62). He was fed up of being alive. Byrony just wanted to go to Valhalla. He had a long life. Byrony went into the damp woods, looking for someone to battle. He searched the perimeter of the land but didn't find anyone. After seven minutes he found a Viking to battle with. He was very buff. He started to sprint down the hill and he tripped over a rock and then stumbled down the hill. So he went to the old house and saw a magic door. It said: *If You Dare - Entrance To Valhalla*. Byrony entered the room and smelt blood. He saw Vikings fighting, having the best time of their lives. So he joined them.

Mia Casson (10)
Monkwray Junior School, Whitehaven

The Mystery Door

Isaac and Milo were such good friends but one day at school a mystery door appeared out of nowhere. "I-I-Isaac, I've never seen that door before..."

"Don't be silly, Milo, it's probably a new door the school's put in."

Milo noticed a sparkle from the door but then suddenly Isaac opened the door and went through. Milo joined him. Milo was shocked to find they weren't in school.

"Isaac!" screamed Milo.

"Milo!" screamed back Isaac.

Then they realised that they were next to each other. "You okay?" they both said and they looked around to see they were in a candy world.

Chloe Davidson (9)
Monkwray Junior School, Whitehaven

The Girl, The Dragon And The Forest

Once, there was a girl called Claire. She lived with her dad and mum. One day, her mum told her not to go to the special door. She usually listened to her mum and dad, however this time she did not listen. She was eager to see it. One night she went peeking outside and she was amazed. She saw the forest and she took some precious treasure when she came to a cave. There was a weird sound. It was a dragon who had a broken leg so she helped the dragon. The dragon was happy so he took her on many rides. She was very happy. She ate her food with the dragon and she told the dragon goodbye and said, "I will meet you next time."

Joan Tryphena Ashwin (9)
Monkwray Junior School, Whitehaven

The Magic Door

Once upon a time, there was a door or shall I say a magic door. A young girl opened the door and it was something nobody had seen before. It was a wonderland. It had mushrooms, hills, waterfalls and even smelly flowers. It was like a dream. The girl could smell roses and all types of things. It was brilliant. The girl could feel the magic on her fingertips. The hillside was beautiful and the mushrooms as well. After that, people found out her name and she had a dog. Her name was Lala and her dog was called Bubby. Later, she made it back through the magic door and nobody has been through it since.

Millie Shaw (9)
Monkwray Junior School, Whitehaven

Ronaldo's History

One day a man called Ronaldo started his career as a teenager. He loved playing football with his best friend. He loved his friend. One day his friend and him saw a Manchester United scout. His friend gave him an assist and he scored.

Cristiano Ronaldo loved his Manchester United career but he signed for Real Madrid until 2019 when he left to play for Juventus. He later went back to United and scored hattricks, penalties and freekicks but he had an argument with the manager and his contract got terminated.

He's still playing now.

Jayden Martin-Nicholson (8)

Monkwray Junior School, Whitehaven

The Door To Space

One day, Archer, a little 10-year-old boy, found a mysterious door in his bedroom. It was gold, iron and silver. He entered the door and found himself in space. He looked down and found himself on Saturn. He loved it! He was amazed. Out of all the planets, Saturn was his favourite planet. He loved the giant ring around it. He found a rocket and blasted to the moon. He thought he was an astronaut. Finally, it was time to go home where he told everyone about his day.

Leo Dobson (10)
Monkwray Junior School, Whitehaven

The Man And The Portal

Once upon a time, there was a man named Ben. He went into town. A mysterious portal appeared. He went inside the portal. It teleported him to a land. There was lots of candy. He went on the path. He found a mysterious treasure chest. He opened it. It was a portal so he jumped into the portal. He went back into town and then home.

Connor Hodgson (9)
Monkwray Junior School, Whitehaven

World Cup Final

When I opened the magic door I could see France and England and in the background, I could see the World Cup. I could see Harry Kane and Kylian Mbappé. There were lots of fans in the stands. I could hear the fans roaring and shouting and singing songs.

Koby Johnston (8)
Monkwray Junior School, Whitehaven

The Forest

When I was in my room a door appeared. I walked through. It was a new world. There were animals and birds. It was so exciting and I wanted to explore so I ran around to see more. I saw a tiger first. I thought it would eat me but it did not. It had hurt its paw. I tried to help but I did not have anything with me.

After a while, it started to get windy. Me and the tiger tried to find a safe place. Later on, we finally found a cave. I made two beds out of leaves and started a fire. When I woke up the magic door appeared in the cave. I opened the door but the tiger did not want me to leave.

I said, "I have to go but I guess you can come with me. Wait here and see."

My mum said, "We cannot have a tiger in our house!"

"Please, Mum, I will take care of it," I said.

"Fine," my mum said.

So I brought the tiger in from the cave and we had lots of fun.

Iona Taylor (7)
Potten End CE Primary School, Potten End

A Magic Winter

One cold night, I skipped out of my bed and I saw a magic door. In a second, it sucked me up. I was swirling in a rainbow tornado. *Poof!* I saw so many snowmen and snowdrops that were falling from the sky. I walked ten steps to the left and I saw a candy cane shop. Right next to that there was a headband shop. I bought one that said 'Ho ho ho'. I loved it but the cold wind blew away my headband. I was pretty sad. It blew into Rudolph's antlers and tangled up his lights but would you believe it, I saw Santa right next to him. He was very jolly. He said, "Is this your headband?" I said, "Yes."

We tried to untangle my headband then I left Santa. I was so surprised when I saw my friend, Lyla. I said, "Merry Christmas." We went out the door together. We also had a playdate.

Lottie Crouch (6)
Potten End CE Primary School, Potten End

Sweetie Land

In my bedroom, I saw a peculiar door. It smelt like sweets and sugar. I almost fainted with excitement. I ran through the door, and shut it behind me with a bang, crash and wallop! I noticed that it was not the door that smelt yummy. It was where I was. There were sweetie clouds, bunnies and sugar air. I could hear clapping and sweetie rain falling to the ground. The bunnies were screaming loudly for a race was about to start. I sat down to watch. I noticed that people were driving sweetie cars. I watched closely and noticed that they pressed a 'go' button which was a pedal and it would just go. They didn't have to keep their foot on the pedal. If they said 'stop' it would stop. When the race ended I saw the people racing were also sweets.

Abbie Swift (6)

Potten End CE Primary School, Potten End

A Trip To Disneyland

One sunny day, I saw a magic door. I went inside and saw a princess welcoming me. I walked through and said, "Thank you."

Suddenly I saw lots of rides. Suddenly I felt very excited. I decided to do something. The first thing I did was go to Belle's castle. It was very fun. Then I did not know what to do. Then I had an idea. My idea was to go on a ride but I did not know what ride. I had to think then I had an idea. I wanted to go on a roller coaster. I found a really fast roller coaster. I went on it. It felt very cool. After that, I went to get some food. I bought candyfloss. It was delicious. Then I went back to the door.

Should I tell someone? It was fun on the adventure but I want to keep it a secret, I thought.

Felicity Roberts (7)

Potten End CE Primary School, Potten End

The Big Roller Coaster

Once, I found a door and stepped inside it. There was a massive roller coaster. I ran around for hours and hours until I found the entrance. When I found it I got on the roller coaster before it got away. I was starting to go up. I was quite scared and then I went down so fast that I nearly fell off. I went on a loopity-loop. When it was finished the door started disappearing fast. But I didn't want to leave so I had a wander around. I could see some more things but there was only that one roller coaster but at that time the magic door was gone so I had to find another way to get out. But there was no other way to get out so I walked around in circles until I was so dizzy I fell over. There wasn't an end so I had to stay at that place.

Spencer South (7)
Potten End CE Primary School, Potten End

The Cold, Magic, Wild Wonder Wood

It started at the door. I just woke up and opened my bedroom door. Then I stumbled somewhere. *Poof! Crash!*
Something moved. Suddenly something else moved. I found out it was the trees. I was scared so I called my mum. This is what I said..."Come, Mother!" I screamed. Then I wanted to explore. I looked and looked for a friend and luckily I found one. It was a hedgehog called Ruby and her friend, Alexandra. I played at a party. Then I had twenty cakes.
The door disappeared and it took one hour to get back. After that, it came and it was midnight.

Sophia Farrington (6)
Potten End CE Primary School, Potten End

The Rainforest Adventure

One morning, I saw a door. I jumped inside. Suddenly I could see animals everywhere. Sunlight was hard to see. I hid for cover under a tree but a jaguar jumped down and started growling. I thought it was a fight. I tried my best to block its blows. Soon I ran away... Was I safe? I heard something and a gorilla jumped on me. I don't know what happened next but everything turned black! I woke up and I was in the trees! Then I was in a boxing ring. I punched the gorilla out of the ring and some gorillas carried me to the door and waved me goodbye.

Marcus Horner (7)
Potten End CE Primary School, Potten End

An Amazing Party

One day I found a rock party! In the trees I climbed and climbed. I visited it and I saw a fire. I did a no-handed cartwheel. Me and my friend Sky played together. We climbed a tree. The tree had hanging sweets. We drew a Christmas tree with sticks. We also made reindeer. We made snowflakes together and built a star in the tree but it was burnt down and we fell on the ground. We made nuts as well. I fell over but Sky helped me up. We opened presents up together. We played school and we dressed up as well.

Skyler Alexander (6)
Potten End CE Primary School, Potten End

Santa's Grotto

I ran up the stairs and into my room. As I opened the cupboard door I wasn't in my room anymore, it was cold and snowy. I saw an elf wrapping presents. I saw Santa. I ran towards him. "Yes! Santa, is it really you? Hi, I'm Heidi, do you want to be friends with me?"

"Yes," he said.

I saw lots of new things. The room was really good. The food was candy. I got to ride Santa's sleigh. It was my last day and I had to go back through the cupboard door.

Heidi Clark (7)
Potten End CE Primary School, Potten End

The Cold North Pole

One day I opened my cupboard and, *poof!* It sucked me up. I opened my eyes and I stuck my tongue out. On my tongue, I felt a snowflake. I was at the North Pole. I walked and walked until I saw a little factory. I stepped inside and I saw some elves. Then I saw someone fat, very fat indeed. He was Santa! I saw Santa with my own eyes! He said, "What are you doing in the cold North Pole? You should go home."

I listened because I did not want coal for Christmas.

Fleur Taylor (6)
Potten End CE Primary School, Potten End

Rainbow Factory

I ran through a door and it closed behind me. I saw a river with a sign saying: *River Rock Woods*. I looked around and saw Blue. He ran for me. I hid in a box. He passed by me. I walked through showers and saw Green, he was blind. I walked on and saw a track, it was Orange! I went in a locker. He ran past me. I ran on. I felt something on my feet. It was Purple's hands. I wiggled them off and got a hammer. I broke the door and escaped.

Ritchie Chillingworth (7)
Potten End CE Primary School, Potten End

Me And The Football Stadium

One day I found a magic door that appeared in the wild. I wondered what was in it so I stepped through it. In the magic door, I saw the Qatar football stadium and I said, "Is that the Qatar football stadium?" I was very excited at first and I didn't know what was coming next...

The next day I stepped into Qatar and I fell out of bed. For a minute I fainted. I rushed to the football stadium and saw the whole World Cup final.

Charles Coventry (7)
Potten End CE Primary School, Potten End

The Book Door

Once, I was going to move house. When I was cleaning I saw a door. I was surprised by it. I walked right into the door. There was a library. It was covered in lots of books. I read lots of the books. I loved it. It had lots of bookshelves. I loved it and then I couldn't believe it, I saw Santa! He was very jolly. After that, I had to go. I was sad that I had to leave but I knew everyone would have fun. Merry Christmas, everyone.

Lyla Gwynne (7)
Potten End CE Primary School, Potten End

The Amazing World Of Sweets

Me and my family were walking. We saw a door. I opened it. There was a flag that said: 'Aaliyah'. "Will I love love the sweets?" I said, eating a marshmallow. There stood a giant honey puddle. I ate that as well. Something strange happened. Every time I ate a sweet another appeared then I screamed because every sweet came to life. I ran to a world the same except the sweets didn't come to life!

Aaliyah Geddes (6)
Potten End CE Primary School, Potten End

Godzilla's Home

Once, there... Wait a minute, it was my birthday! I was having a swimming party. When I got there I walked to a door but it kept trying to get me. It was the same size as myself. It grabbed me and pulled me in. I was in the sea. There I was in Godzilla's home! He was kind, he said, "Go home and also, happy birthday."
I went through the door and said, "Goodbye."

Cassius Horner (7)
Potten End CE Primary School, Potten End

Easter Hunt

I opened the door. I was on an Easter egg hunt.
Suddenly I was in a race. I barely got any eggs. I
was so angry. I ran to the finish line but I was the
last one. I was so sad.

Then I ran to the magic door... I had lots of sweets.
Then I ran back. I got lots of eggs. I was so happy.
Every day I had lots of sweets. I was living happily.
I love my life!

Sky Wiggan (6)

Potten End CE Primary School, Potten End

Welcome To Fairyland

One frosty, cold day I went through a frozen door. *Poof!* I saw lots of fairies and pixies. I went into a magic door! I had a lot of fun. In the end, they asked me to go home (they'd had enough of me!). I did go back. The magic door sparkled. I was back in my bedroom. *Magic!* I thought. After that, I went straight to sleep.

Ava Whiting (7)
Potten End CE Primary School, Potten End

Exciting Lapland

One sunny morning, I ran through a door. Wow! It was Lapland. Right behind me there was a flying reindeer. It was freezing and there were more than 2,000 candy canes. I felt Santa's beard. I heard lots of snow falling and saw a snowman. I saw lots of carrots then I felt tired so I went through the door and went to bed.

Phoebe Deaton (6)
Potten End CE Primary School, Potten End

The Magic Door

One cold day, I saw a magic door. I stepped in the door. It was the North Pole! It was so cold. I saw an elf. I said, "Hi, let's explore!"
I saw Rudolph. He was cute. I got to ride on him. After that, I saw Santa. He gave me some magic. "I need to go now but I will be back, bye!"

Vienna-Violet Green (7)
Potten End CE Primary School, Potten End

The Incredible World Cup

Once, one day, I was in my garden when I saw a door. It was magic. When I stepped in I suddenly found myself at the World Cup final. The score was 9-0 and the crowd were roaring. Then it was half-time... The football fell to my feet. I kicked it and I scored. The crowd roared!

Hugo Harrap (6)
Potten End CE Primary School, Potten End

The Souls Don't Dare To Step In

An extract

A magic door. A door that souls don't dare to step in... No, not even an inch. This so-called 'magical door' isn't like any other ordinary door. No. It's not like those little, magical fantasy books aimed at children 8-9 years old where the protagonist gets transported somewhere magical - it's the exact opposite. Did you know there was a rumour about a young innocent youth who stepped into this so-called magical door full of mysteries and never came back? The story will leave you in pure devastation! Once upon a time, a young, unfortunate girl named Sara was playing in the luscious emerald field, where the magic door stood waiting to lure someone in, as fresh air filled her lungs like a glass cup waiting to be filled with a cold beverage. After a long time, she unexpectedly noticed a withered, ancient-looking door standing impatiently as if it was waiting for something. Curious. Baffled. Puzzled. She slowly yet cautiously strolled towards this magical door. What was going to happen? Was she that absent-minded to step in? Was she going to die?

134

As she innocently strolled towards the magic door her silky, black hair dangled elegantly from her head to her shoulders like a waterfall. Finally, she was in front of the magic door. What was her next move? Run away or step in...?

After a couple of minutes, she knew she had to make a decision as the blazing inferno was setting on the horizon, creating a picturesque scene. This was a truly life-or-death situation. Sara slowly raised her hand and clenched on the gold doorknob. Was she really going to risk her life for some door?

Zeenat Noori
Waterside Primary School, Hanley

The Door

He looked around to see nothing, except for a door. A door that could lead to anything. He cautiously walked towards the door. he looked into the endless black void. Nothing. Nothing at all. He grew more anxious. He mustered all the courage he had, trembling all the way. His legs felt like noodles, his mind ran to intrusive thoughts. Then he did it...

He stepped through the door to see something extraordinary. He saw a colosseum-like structure and crowds of ecstatic people in robes - something immensely different from the city where he was from. Letting curiosity get the better of him, he cautiously strode toward it. The people quickly rushed to some seats. This is Ludas and his story. Ludas rushed towards an empty seat, trying not to bring too much attention. Two people ran into the middle of the arena, at the bottom. As the ecstatic crowd cheered, the commentator yelled, "And for the last competitors of the competition we have..." The roars of the people grew louder and louder... "We have Txan of Pugnatar and Harrius of Anglia."

Some guards marched toward the two people and handed them an item. One had a brilliant, aquamarine blade and the other had a sword, that looked as hot as the sun. The crowd let out an uproarious cheer.

Everyone was ecstatic and happy. Everyone from 8-year-olds to 80-year-olds were cheering and smiling. Suddenly a deafening and nonhuman sound came. A coal-black gas-looking creature flew through the stadium. Not long after the chug of a train arrived and an ear-piercing horn blew from afar...

Cato Conibear (10)

Waterside Primary School, Hanley

Indigo's Magic Door Adventure

One morning, in a magical place, there lived a boy called Indigo, he was very kind and loved studying the ocean which means coral reefs, sea animals, bacteria and much more such as temperatures of the seas and cephalopods.

It was a sunny morning, and the rays of sunlight beamed on the window of his room. As the alarm clock rang he exhaustedly got out of bed and put his clothes on. He rapidly ran down the stairs whilst holding his pale hand on the dusty, wooden railing.

"Mom, is breakfast ready?" asked Indigo excitedly because he loved food.

"It's ready, honey," his mother replied.

When Indigo reached downstairs at the table he realised it was all wet. "Mum, why is it wet?" he sadly questioned.

"Oh, forgot to tell you, your dad washed the house," his mother answered.

"Where am I going to eat now?" he cried.

"The basement," she replied.

He walked down the creaky staircase until, *splash!* He dropped his cereal when he reached the bottom. "Urgh!" he moaned.

Even though he had only been in the basement a few times he thought something was wrong. There was never a door there before. Suddenly a purple glow came from behind the door. *What's behind there?* he thought. He put his hand on the doorknob...

It opened. He thought he was in a dream. Indigo was speechless. There were coral reefs, sea animals, currents, eels, turtles, fish, sponges, and everything else that was in the ocean.

Ianis Papuse (8)

Waterside Primary School, Hanley

The Magic Door

Once upon a time, there lived a little girl called Olivia. One winter's day, Olivia was very bored, so she decided to go on a walk in the woods as she wanted an adventure. In the middle of the woods, there was a door, Olivia was curious, so she opened the door and inside was a beautiful rainforest. She then realised the door was a magic door full of exciting creatures and places to explore. She could see a toucan with its coal-coloured feathers and his multicoloured beak. He was squawking so loudly that it hurt Olivia's ears. She also saw a brown, fluffy monkey acting mischievously because he was stealing bananas from the tall trees. Olivia felt excited, surprised and enchanted by this magical rainforest. The sun shone brightly overhead in the morning sky, it was beaming through the emerald-green trees. She walked a little further, small twigs crunching under her tiny feet. She came face-to-face with a lemur, who had a long black and white striped tail. He took one look at Olivia and ran away further into the rainforest.

Olivia thought she should go home before she ventured even further and got lost. She found her way back through the greenery, back to the door she came from. She closed the magic door and went back home feeling happy but tired after her adventurous day. The next day when Olivia woke up she decided she would go through the door and explore further. She got to the woods where the door was, excited to meet more animals but the door had magically disappeared.

Madison Wainwright (8)

Waterside Primary School, Hanley

The Wonderland Where Everything Grows

I opened the magic door to find the most beautiful place I have ever seen. It has snow falling through the sky and hovering above the ground. The snowflakes are rainbows. You can feel a soft breeze coming through the air and it really feels amazing on your cheek. You can hear the birds singing sweet songs that have high and low-pitched notes. The trees are evergreen and all of the birds come and rest in their long, brown branches.

The land has beautiful houses with rainbows in every window and snowflakes on the roof. When it comes to Christmas you can feel the warmth coming from inside each house. Each one has gorgeous lights that twinkle in the night sky. Some houses have pink and white lights, but others have blue and green lights. This is the home of elves and good goblins. They have the most unusual pets! Some goblins have rainbow dragons and the elves have the biggest butterflies anyone has ever seen. Some goblins don't have dragons though, they keep unicorns that have pink bodies, multicoloured horns and blue hair with white spots.

On Thursdays, goblins take their pets to training so they can be the best they can be. Dragons are trained to be garden protectors because they have big, mighty wings to fly up and see in the distance. Unicorns are trained to help goblins who need it most.

This truly is an amazing winter wonderland.

Sophie Smith (7)

Waterside Primary School, Hanley

Princess And The Giants

Once upon a time, a little girl found a magic door. The little girl opened the door slowly and it started to glow. As the little girl looked behind the door she saw meandering, towering trees. The sky was gloomy and dark and the clouds were heavy. She felt nervous as she walked in and saw a huge, tall castle poking out above the trees. A princess was walking elegantly out of the castle. She had long ginger hair and a purple flowered dress. The little girl followed her on her walk to find friends. The princess found a family of giants - Mr Giant, Mrs Giant and Miss Giant.

Miss Giant and the princess went swimming in a lake and had a picnic. Just then the little girl snatched Miss Giant away. The princess felt sad, she had tears in her eyes. She ran home as quickly as she could but when she got home the queen was gone because she was looking for the princess. Then the queen saw a giant castle. She got a bit closer but she was too close and she got caught. The princess went to the giant castle. When she got there she spoke to the guards and they let her in. The princess found the queen and set her free.

They went back home to drop the queen back and then the princess went to check outside. Then she saw Miss Giant. She let her in. They lived happily ever after.

Ellia Ratcliffe (7)
Waterside Primary School, Hanley

The Magic Door

Dashing, running, her long brown hair flowing in the wind. Imani, a forgotten, abandoned girl, had been trying to run away for years, as she was overshadowed by society, left all alone to fend for herself.

As she ran and sprinted, she ran closer to the horizon, as if she had reached the edge of the world. As she stopped to catch her breath, without warning, a mysterious door summoned in front of her. The closer she got to it, the brighter a mystical light shone before her. Temptation swallowing her up, she dived inside, as she was engulfed in a vibrant light. The second she set foot outside her abnormal adventure, a mesmerising glow of purple hit her face, enchanting the whole new world, which was a forest, lively and bright. As she strolled around the new universe, she heard the crunch of grass, and animals scurrying at her feet. "What a majestic forest," she exclaimed with delight. As she rested her mind, gazing at the twinkling stars in the midnight sky, faint whispers and buzzing wings could be heard in the distance.

Creeping closer and closer to investigate, spontaneously an eye-catching fairy appeared. Although this was hectic, she knew she would never be seen in the public eye again.

Jesme Kassai (10)
Waterside Primary School, Hanley

The Magic Door

A long time ago, far far away, there lived an old lady. Next to her snug, wooden cottage there was a flowing, clear river. The river was as long as a snake. Whenever she looked at the river she could remember all the good times she had. One day she was strolling on the cobbled, stony path next to the cobbled, stony path. There was a trickling, sparkling river, it led to something mysterious. All of a sudden, she fell into a well. There were rows of doors. "Argh! Help me, I am drowning, help, help!" she shouted loudly.

Unusually she arrived somewhere magical. It was a colourful, fresh garden that had delicate, vivid flowers, they were so eye-catching. Each flower had a different power when the old, kind-hearted lady touched a magenta rose a cute, petite bird came out of it. Beautiful butterflies hovered above the wildflowers. She touched many more flowers like red, violet, yellow, orange and many more. She wanted to go home and all of a sudden she was back to her cottage.

Aisha Qasimi (9)
Waterside Primary School, Hanley

The Wonders Of The Door

What lies behind the magical door is left for many to decide for themselves. Once your curiosity takes over you and you decide to enter through the door there is no going back. What lies behind this door will shock you to your core. An isolated troll lives and viciously rocks itself back and forth until it falls asleep. Its beady eyes and pupils are surrounded by red and it makes a noise every time it blinks. Surprisingly, this beady-eyed creature is not what it seems, in fact, this troll will play with you if you're nice of course and sometimes he will make a joke or two. See, first impressions are not everything. He also has a mystical hut that no one dares enter in case a fiery wrath enters the fun atmosphere that occurs. Some people feel wary even if they have gotten to know the troll personally but some people trust the troll even after their first impression of him.

Brianna Chadwick (10)
Waterside Primary School, Hanley

Candyland

I was so excited because I was going to Candyland today. When I was travelling to Candyland I saw a magical rainbow. It was so bright that my eye was starting to watch. When I went past the rainbow I finally arrived. I was super excited that I rapidly ran towards the raining cotton candy. I got my basket and tried to catch it. It was so hard but I managed to get 20 cotton candy canes. When the beautiful sunset came I saw a lollipop stand and I went to buy the Coca-Cola lollipop. When I finished my lollipop I had to go home. When I was going home I just remembered the rainbow and the rainbow just reminds me of Candyland.

I really enjoyed Candyland but now it is past my bedtime. When I arrived I quietly went to my comfy, soft bed. When I fell asleep I dreamt about Candyland. I wish I could go back to Candyland.

Sabahat Amanyar (8)
Waterside Primary School, Hanley

The Magic Door

Once, there was a secret, magical passageway leading to a spectacular wonderland. It had alicorns, myths and fairies too. It also had the most beautiful castle ever. King Henry and Queen Mary owned the palace a thousand years ago. Since then their family have lived in the kingdom of Kestopia!

Every year, on the 5th of January, the kingdom's people celebrate their kingdom, the king and the queen. On that day the people paint some drawings and every year there is something different. There is joy and laughter everywhere and even a giant cake. This cake is usually the size of an armchair. Every 10th of April there is also a celebration to bring good luck and love to everyone. Dragons only come on that day. I really wish I get a chance to go to Kestopia one day. If only I could find the magic door...

Lara Bernardes (8)
Waterside Primary School, Hanley

A Realm Of Magic

As the magic door opened, a blurry image appeared in front of me. Fluffy, pink cotton candy clouds danced all around me with elegance, while the wind whistled and flew past me. Wondering what this mysterious place was, I then took one step and began to have a feeling of excitement. I met an elegant fairy, Anna. She took me to the pink castle nearby. I saw a small stable holding a horse with a horn and it was a rainbow, majestic unicorn named Sophia. She neighed. I climbed on her back then we burst into the pink castle. All of a sudden, I saw a gleaming light shining ever so brightly. It was a treasure chest. Excitedly, I opened it and a bunch of sparkly diamonds lay in it.

A light turned on and I saw my mum. I thought, *was it all a dream?*

Aisha Hannah Isa Hafizs (6)
Waterside Primary School, Hanley

Is It The End?

Once upon a time, I was collecting diamonds, emeralds and gold in the abandoned mine. I collected enough to craft my armour set. I was so excited to put on my armour. Just then I saw a flash of bright light. In front of me was a magic door sparkling in the lamplight. I opened the door and was sucked through a portal. It took me to the Nether.

I had to fight the wither skeletons with my diamond sword. I started to feel cold all over. Spooky sounds whistled past my ears. I spun around and saw ten Endermen charging at me. I fought them all bravely. I entered the stronghold and finally found the end portal where I passed through and faced my final battle.

I slayed the Enderdragon and saved the Overworld.

Myles Logan (6)

Waterside Primary School, Hanley

A Walk Into The Future

When I opened the mysterious door I saw the future where new things were invented. I also could see that the door was covered in purple and had pixie dust.

When I entered I could hear the buzzing sound of the flying cars and the roaring sound of the jetpacks. I could feel the hard, smooth and bright walls of the skyscrapers.

I am happy that I have had the chance to see the fascinating future, however, I have to escape back through the magic door to the 21st century where I am living now.

Mikael Mohd Zaid (8)

Waterside Primary School, Hanley

The Not-So-Ordinary Door

Imagine, there is a magic door in front of you... Will you open it to see treasure or magical animals or will there be a portal to an unknown land? Will it be an exciting adventure or will it be a strange adventure with some amazing twists to it? Or maybe, just maybe, you will travel to a place that you can't help yourself stop exploring and you will run into some unbelievable secrets. Will you magically go to a world which was in the past? Will you open the door? Will you ever get out?

Gabriel Gaisie (7)
Waterside Primary School, Hanley

Winter Wonderland

One day I went to Winter Wonderland and I had lots of fun. And when the people screamed my ears started to hurt. When I went on a ride I started getting butterflies in my tummy. Whilst I was walking I saw a homeless person. I gave him 20p. He began to smile whilst I was leaving. When I left I found a ride that was so scary. It went upside down. I thought I would fall down. After that, I went on another ride, it gave me goosebumps. I was so dizzy. After that, I went home and got in my bed.

Asra Amanyar (6)
Waterside Primary School, Hanley

The New Pirate Land

Once upon a time, there was a new pirate land and I travelled there from miles away. The place was so exciting. I found some strange sea creatures. I saw a big scary sea animal and I ran away. Then I moved on along the shore. I saw a few pirates running around and having fun. As I went on a pirate ship I explored a treasure chest. It was full of jewels and precious stones. The pirate land was full of adventure and it was so amazing.

Muneeb Shaikh (7)

Waterside Primary School, Hanley

The Magic Door

Once upon a time, there lived a little girl called Jocelyn. She went to a treasure island. She got there by going through a door, not just any door but a magic door that transported her. She took all of her friends and her mum and dad to have fun with. She saw a palm tree and climbed up it to get some coconuts for her mum, dad and friends. Then something scary happened, it got stormy. So she went back through the magic door.

Jocelyn Williams (7)
Waterside Primary School, Hanley

The Rainforest Adventure

I explore new animals that I haven't seen in a long time and I see what the rainforest looks like.
Before I go and explore the rainforest I need my supplies.
I take my camera because I can take pictures so I can remember the animals. I can also use a light so I can see in the dark.
Rainforest is my favourite place in the world. There are lots of things to explore and I love to explore a lot of new things.

Antonia Cernat (8)
Waterside Primary School, Hanley

The Mysterious Door

In my bedroom, there is a mysterious door. Would you like to know where it goes? I will tell you. It leads to a magical forest full of trees and bushes. There are some strange smells and some lovely smells. Some come from withered trees and black roses. The lovely smells come from pop-pop flowers. Oh, and the coolest animal is the dino-corn (half dinosaur, half unicorn). All fun!

Millie Ellis (6)
Waterside Primary School, Hanley

The Magic Door

I wish, when I open my magic door, it takes me to London. I want to see Big Ben and the London Eye. I want to see Buckingham Palace because the Queen used to live in that palace. I want to sit on the tourist bus and see the whole city of London. This is my best time to spend in London. I am so excited to explore London. I love London! I love the Queen!

Zarnish Imtiaz (6)
Waterside Primary School, Hanley

Lily And The Room Of Cuteness

Long ago, this young child went home and unlocked the door but as she merrily walked through she saw cute little kittens playing with wool and pandas eating bamboo.
The thing was these were no ordinary creatures, these fluffballs were mythical and granted you any three wishes you'd like.
This was a dream come true.

Lily Upton (7)
Waterside Primary School, Hanley

162

Deal With The Demon

At 4:50 in the afternoon, Evie was in bed in her room. It seemed mysterious. She heard a sound coming from her closet. She opened her closet and she got pulled in. "Where am I?" There was a feeling of torture. "I think it is the gate of Heaven and Hell. I want to go home!"

The angel said, "Hi, do not make a deal with a demon."

The next day she forgot. "Hi. My name is Evie."

"Go away or make a deal with me! The deal is to stay here and I'll tell your family that you're okay. Just kidding, the actual deal is you must not leave until you are sixteen years old."

"That won't be for two years."

"Sorry. Not sorry! You have to stay here for two years. I'm changing my mind, you can stay here for one year, now go to bed. I will let you sleep," said the demon.

"I want to go home," said Evie.

Day 103... I am going home. I need to wait until the demon is asleep. He is asleep. I have to go home now. It is so hot. I think I might pass out. I need to go. I'm out of here! I miss my mum.

Zia Clarck (10)

Woodburn Primary School, Dalkeith

Nightmare Land

One dark, gloomy day there was a boy, a bag and his pet gigantic lizard that had lost all its power in a big fight. He could ride it everywhere. He rode it like a bike and the lizard liked spicy sandwiches. Then one day, the lizard started to glow. It was gleaming but it looked a bit sluggish. It looked determined to do something so the boy followed. They reached a door that led into fog and they saw waterfalls, grass fields and trees with crystals. The boy was confused, he didn't know what the phenomenon was then he saw that the crystals started to glow so bright that they almost blinded them. They ran. All was dark and gloomy. They were terrified. They hid and saw, well, I can't really explain. It was rolling and bashing the rocks. The place we were hiding in was incredible, it was filled with coloured rocks. Suddenly we saw a monkey that looked drunk. It jumped down and smashed the ground with a big punch. It smashed the ground and started to chase us at an incredible pace.

We escaped and took shelter in a bunker. The monkey smashed into the door and continuously punched it until it died. The next day we went exploring around and saw a pale white creature that had red eyes, it was disturbing to look at then we saw that its limbs looked like they were broken but they weren't so I summoned a dog to fight it off. When it caught up to us it tried to drown me but I heard a loud crunching noise. It alarmed the creature but it didn't have the strength.
We decided to try and escape the nightmare land. We called a helicopter and escaped.

Noah McFarlane (10)
Woodburn Primary School, Dalkeith

The Tropical Rainforest

Walking in the woods, I saw a door. Feeling excited I burst through it to the other side. I was amazed because I saw a tropical rainforest. "Wow!" As I was looking around I saw a wooden bridge. Crossing the bridge I lost my footing and fell through a gap. Just in time, I caught the bridge. "Help!" Suddenly a panda and a girl, Sophia, appeared and pulled me up. "Thanks for saving me," I exclaimed.

The girl smiled and gestured for me to follow. We reached a treehouse and I realised the panda hadn't followed us. "Oh no, we need to go back."

"No! Just wait until the morning."

"But I'm really tired."

"Fine, I'm going to find the panda." But I could not find him anywhere.

"Pssst! Here, I'm down by the river."

"Oh, hi, what are you?"

"I'm a tropical fish."

"Oh, you're my favourite fish that ever existed."

"Thanks but what do you need?"

"I need to find a panda."

"Oh yes, I found a panda over there by a magical door."

"Uh-oh, I need to get him." But when I did he almost fell in.

"Oh my goodness, look, Ava, there is a wood on the other side of this door. I want to go in."

"No! Stop! That's the wood near my house."

"Oh, okay, you go in." He pushed me back into the woods.

Ava McPhee (10)
Woodburn Primary School, Dalkeith

Portal Story

One long, boring day at school Jack was walking his usual way home. When he turned a corner, a door standing there perfectly still like a human. Jack was confused, *who left it there?* he wondered. It was decorated with all sorts of candy gumdrops, chewy sweets and all sorts of icing. Jack curiously opened the door.

Fluffy pink cotton candy trees were the first thing Jack saw. In amazement, he stood up. He could smell fresh gingerbread men getting made followed by a sweet scent leading to who knows where. While following the scent he saw giant lollipops and suckers, it felt like any child's dream. He saw sticky gumdrops and gummy bears.

Jack finally stumbled across the scent but it was a gingerbread house. It looked like a friendly house beautifully decorated with gumdrops and icing and tasty refreshing-looking peppermints. It had gummy bear gnomes and macaroon fences with cute faces carved into them. He entered to find gingerbread people living inside. There was a little brother and a middle child and of course, there was an older brother. The oldest brother told him not to go too deep into the forest. Jack thanked the brothers and left.

Jack couldn't resist going too deep into the forest. He passed through the candy cane field and trekked through swamps. Then he finally came across an old-looking hut overflowing with vines and moss. It turned out that was the door back home, then he opened it...

Joshua Tennant (10)
Woodburn Primary School, Dalkeith

Three Islands Of Randomness

Nathan is an ordinary boy from England with dyed red hair with a strand of blue through it and glasses... but one time he wasn't ordinary and nobody knew. Nathan was just coming home from school when he saw a door he hadn't seen before. With his curiosity, he opened it.

He went through and he was on a raft but he got seasick. "Did somebody cast a spell like 'luck be gone' or something?"

Then a random goat appeared saying, "Where you wanna go, Carthnia, Nutrland or... nah?"

"Nutrland," answered Nathan.

They arrived and saw fruit and vegetables. Then a strawberry walked up to him and said, "If you're going to the third island make sure you know how to attack!"

Then Nathan went exploring and found lots of food. "This is boring," said Nathan. "Take me to Carthnia!"

They arrived and they saw tons of gingerbread men and candy. "This place looks awesome!"

"I wouldn't be too sure about that," said a tiny lollipop. "We've just been invaded by the third island so many of us have been crumpled!"
"I'll stop them!" said Nathan with gritted teeth. "Take me to the third island!" Then they started going to the third island.
He arrived and tried using karate and noticed that he didn't know karate and he then woke up in his bed.

Adam McKechnie (9)
Woodburn Primary School, Dalkeith

The 1960s

One day I was filming the new movie 'Blast From The Past'. At lunch break, I walked into the kitchen, noticing that the door looked different. They probably just painted it but it looked exciting. Half of it was dotty and the other half was chequered. Walking through the door I realised it wasn't the kitchen anymore. It was an exciting, dancing musical room. All of a sudden, everybody froze and looked at me. You could hear a pin drop in the silence. When the music started (I think it was Elvis or The Beatles), I didn't know what to do. I was scared so I took a line from the movie and said, "Let's rock and roll all night round." I could hear people agreeing with me.

Someone came over and asked me to dance. I said, "Yes, but I don't know who you are!"

They suddenly announced, "I'll make you some friends, my sister's looking for some. She is awesome." He said 'awesome' in a different tone from the rest. I didn't know why but I was scared...

The doors of the bar opened, and everybody scattered to make a path but what was I doing standing in the middle of that path? "That's my sister," said the stranger.

She started walking but when she got to me she pushed me back through the door. When I was gone I could hear them arguing but I didn't mind, I was back just in time for filming.

Amie McGuire (10)
Woodburn Primary School, Dalkeith

Chloe And The Witch

One day, Chloe was playing in her room when her mum asked her to come downstairs. She started walking down when her mum said, "Go outside." So Chloe decided to go for a run in the field. When she got there she noticed a strange door with vegetables and mud splattered on it. Chloe entered the door.

She appeared on an island. It was hot but it was completely deserted. She changed into a swimsuit and started swimming. She decided to go to sleep on the sunbed.

Suddenly, a witch named Clarissa appeared. She had hair as brown as a tree's wood. She whispered to Chloe, "Do not go into the woods." Chloe nodded and Clarissa disappeared.

Later on, Chloe was playing football when the ball rolled into the woods. Chloe chased it. She found a hut in the woods. It had ivy growing on the wall. Chloe went inside. As the door creaked open she noticed a figure staring at her. It took Chloe a moment to realise that it was Clarissa but she looked like she was in her 70s and her hair was white. She shouted, "I told you to stay out of the woods!"

Chloe knew that she needed to get out of there so she ran out but Clarissa wouldn't give up and followed her on a broomstick. She reached the door and ran home.

When she got home Chloe put her hand in her pocket and realised that she had Clarissa's cauldron. Chloe never found the door again.

Abbie Rowe (10)

Woodburn Primary School, Dalkeith

Christmas Wonderland

I was playing hide-and-seek with my friend when I hid in the closet. Peeking through the closet door, I lost my balance and tumbled down into a mysterious, loud, creaky door. My eyes started to shake and I saw a huge amount of rainbow lights. When I looked around, my eyes started to gleam with colourful light. I couldn't believe it, I was in a Christmas wonderland. I saw elves building toys, packing Santa's sack and wrapping presents. I saw a door with light shining out of the keyhole and with no hesitation, I walked in. It was Santa! He was packing his sack for Christmas Day. Suddenly he turned his back and spotted me. "Oh, what are you doing here, young child?" asked Santa.

"Well, I was playing hide-and-seek with my friend and I hid in the closet, then I lost my balance and tumbled into an old creaky door," I replied.

"Let me show you around," said Santa.

He showed me the magical lights, and decorations and even showed me how he makes glittery, cold, fuzzy snow. As we got back to his grotto I said to Santa, "I've got to go, my mum will be wondering where I've been."

"Oh that's fine, remember to always be nice," said Santa.
"Sure will," I replied.
So I walked back to the loud creaky door covered in snow and dashed home as fast as I could. What a wonderful day!

Robbie Hamilton (10)
Woodburn Primary School, Dalkeith

Johnny And The Magic Door

When a boy named Johnny was walking back from football training he saw a black and white chequered door that looked like a chessboard. He opened the door and entered. He had ended up on a strange planet in a city. He began walking through the streets of what looked like a ghost town. He noticed a sign that said: *Welcome To Flying Crab Land*. He was very confused.

When Johnny was exploring the new planet he saw something flying towards him. Strangely it was a flying metal square with four fans on each side keeping it flying. It kept coming closer. Amazingly it spoke and said, "Hello," to Johnny.

"What am I doing here?" he replied.

"Don't steal the crown!" it replied, ignoring Johnny's question.

As he continued his journey in the big city he saw a house. It was unbelievably fancy with a golden roof and diamond floors. The door was unlocked. He slowly opened the gigantic door and saw a crown. It was ruby and gold with a bright blue diamond in the middle.

Suddenly, it started flying all over the place and was shooting lasers. Johnny snatched the crown and ran away. Something appeared in the distance, it was a black hole. Giant volcanoes erupted, everything was being destroyed. He opened the door and ran. He would never find the door again. At that moment Johnny realised he had brought back the crown...

Ben Barnes (9)
Woodburn Primary School, Dalkeith

Deep In The Jungle

One night I woke up feeling nauseous because I kept hearing mysterious noises. I got out of bed and in front of me was a beautiful bright green door covered in ivy and vines. Curiously, I knocked on the door and heard nothing but a monkey noise. I opened the door and I heard, "Oo-ahh."
I jumped off my feet! I nearly had a heart attack! Not believing my ears, I responded, "Argh!"
An orangutan was in front of me, dancing and talking! "Hello, my name is Bob, would you like to explore?" the creature in front of me asked.
I was petrified. I had never talked to an orangutan before. "Where do you want to take me?" I asked nervously.
He responded, "Around the jungle!"
I agreed even though I was cautious.
I entered the jungle and Bob took me straight to the river where crocodiles, pelicans and fish were. I had never seen so much beauty.
There was a small rickety bridge that I walked over and fed some tuna and goldfish. It was amazing!
"Well, I will let you explore," Bob said.

I walked over to the trees and spotted wonderful bluebirds and robins. I ran into Bob again and he had made hot chocolate. He then led me over to the treehouse that he made out of bamboo. I sat down on the comfy puffy couch and enjoyed my hot chocolate, looking at the wonderful view. I felt peaceful.

Sophia Goodwin (10)
Woodburn Primary School, Dalkeith

Dessert Island!

I opened the magic door and it took me to the Atlantic Ocean. That is what I could see.

There were two pirates sailing on the sea. That night a colossal thunderstorm came. They weren't expecting it so they started to panic. A few seconds later the choppy water swallowed up the boat and they landed on an island. Not long after, they woke up. They were both very confused. All they could hear was screeching monkeys, they decided to find shelter and then in the morning they would look for something to eat.

In the morning... they started to look for something to eat because they were starving. They couldn't find any food but they thought that if the monkeys were still alive then there would be food. They spied on the monkeys to see what they were eating.

They were eating the dirt! They tried some because it did smell like cake so they tried some on the count of three. One, two... They were so eager that on three they stuffed it in their mouths! It was amazing! It tasted like chocolate fudge cake.

They tried some other natural things around there. The monkeys were also drinking out of a waterfall so they tried some. *Yum!* they both thought. *This tastes like strawberry milkshake!*

"Peter, could this be the rare dessert island?" said one of the pirates.

"I think it might be," said the other...

Erin Casserly (10)
Woodburn Primary School, Dalkeith

Dragon Hill

One dark, stormy day, Harris was getting chased by a gang. He was running through puddles, the rain was pelting down, Harris was soaking. He saw something, it was a door, it looked like it was in a crime scene, he had never seen it before. The gang was catching up to Harris, so he barged through. While Harris was exploring he stumbled into someone. The stranger said, "I have come to warn you, you cannot stay for over six hours or you will be stuck here forever and after that the only way to escape is to go to Dragon Cave, and kill a dragon!" Harris went to explore.

First, he found some fruit on a tree, it was blue and purple. So Harris ate it, not knowing if it was poisonous or not... After that, he went into the forest and saw some amazing creatures. Finally, he lay down for a nap... When he finally woke up he walked to the door. Harris tried to open it but it was locked. At that second he knew he was too late.

Harris blasted to the dragon cave and entered. There was a massive turquoise dragon roaming around. It was dark and gloomy with bones everywhere. Harris emerged with his shield and dagger and blasted the dragon, which began to bleed gold. Harris grabbed a horn and went through the door.

When Harris returned to his house, Harris was really only away for 30 human minutes. Harris always remembered it by the dragon horn.

Harris Diamond (10)

Woodburn Primary School, Dalkeith

The Winter Village

One morning, Chloe was strolling down to the shops when she suddenly stumbled across a door. The door was made of shiny oak and had vines slithering across the door.

Chloe cautiously opened the mystery door. As she started to walk into the tunnel she heard a joyful voice laughing. Then a figure appeared, it had a ruby-red ribbon in her long brown hair and had a beautiful lime-coloured dress with blood-red dots. At the last step out the tunnel it looked amazing! Snow was gently falling from the sky. It was soft as fluff and smelled of cinnamon.

Chloe saw a shop named 'the workshop'. There was a conveyor belt with wrapped presents. Chloe spotted a mood ring and put it on. A black elf gave her a dirty look as a friendly elf ran away. "Don't steal the Christmas mood ring," he shouted... but she could not remove it!

Then Chloe ran as fast as she could and went to the north side of the village and pulled the massive candy cane. There was a big rumble and the ground started to suddenly shake like an earthquake. Quickly Chloe ran back to the workshop for shelter.

Chloe turned to realise that the door was closing. As Chloe ran she picked up a candy cane and bolted through the door to make it in time. She raced through the door and glanced at her mood ring... Blue for calm! She was still so stunned about what happened.

Mylie Redpath Hamilton (10)
Woodburn Primary School, Dalkeith

Death's Door

In one of the darkest parts of Mexico, Sergeant Dawn was on a mission (Operation Capture). He walked upon an alley of death and saw a mysterious door that he had not seen before. It was wrapped in police tape to cover the horror behind it...

Sergeant Dawn carefully opened this mysterious door and he analysed the area and, to his surprise, he saw land and a ferocious storm in the distance. Dawn felt a hard push on his back. He fell into the mysterious land and saw a black silhouette behind the door saying, "Do not talk to anyone."

The door slammed shut and the portal disappeared. The storm was coming...

He walked for miles until he reached a village. With no caution, he ran into the mysterious village.

He looked around the village but saw nobody and suddenly he heard footsteps behind him, *clat, clat, clat...* A dark silhouette came out from the dark, misty corner. A lady appeared. Dawn said to the lady, "What will stop the storm?"

The promise was broken. The lady turned into a monster. Snakes hissed on her head and there were holes in her body.

He quickly dashed to pick up a stick from the ground and plunged it into the monster's heart. She fell to the ground and inside the heart was a crystal. He pointed it to the storm. *Bang!* He was out of the land but he was in the future...

Isaac Uwagbole (10)

Woodburn Primary School, Dalkeith

The Magic Door

Vladimir was a very violent person. He was part of the KGB. His babushka made lovely borscht, pierogies, oh yes and his babushka got him an AK-47 for his birthday. One day, Vladimir was walking through his office and found a black door that had never been there before. He walked towards it and opened it. He walked through the door and appeared on an island.

Within seconds, a man wearing a dark green tunic appeared. The man had a fluent German accent. He told Vladimir to leave a monster called Figure alone otherwise he would be punished. He also told Vladimir that the creature lived in a library right in the middle of an old Soviet government building and no one knew how it got there. Vladimir was walking through the island's forests when he saw an old Soviet building.

He walked into the building when he saw the library. He ran into the door and the door fell. Vladimir was face-to-face with the monster called Figure. Vladimir shot Figure with his pistol, then he heard something charging towards him. He ran as fast as he could towards the portal that took him there. When he looked behind him he saw the thing that was chasing him.

It was a gigantic man with eight legs. He finally got to the portal and went through. When he got through the portal he found himself in his office in the same place where he went through the door...

Alexander Wrobel MacPhee (10)
Woodburn Primary School, Dalkeith

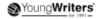

The Door That Led To The Sea

One day, Rose was walking in the woods when she saw a door. Water leaked out from underneath the door and there were cracks in-between the door and the door frame. Water was pouring out of the keyhole like a miniature waterfall! There was a puddle of water beneath the door out of which seaweed grew. Rose decided to open the door and see where it went. She reached out, grabbed the handle and opened the door. She felt her feet leave the ground. It was a weird sensation to be standing still but shooting through time or space or whatever the swirling mist that was surrounding her was. When she reached out to touch it, it moved away.

Eventually, with a loud splash, she landed head-first in the sea and got a great surprise. She was definitely underwater but she was also breathing so she was very confused. Nothing was making sense at all. First, there was the portal and the mist and now there was the ability to breathe underwater which was just plain weird. To add to all that she had no idea where she was.

As Rose swam she saw fish and strange plant-like things that were more like animals. Then she spotted the door. It looked leafy and tree-like. Rose decided this was too strange and opened the door. When the mist vanished she was once again in the woods and the door had vanished, just like the mist had done before it.

Bethan Clelland (10)
Woodburn Primary School, Dalkeith

The Magic Door

One day Dwayne is walking in Glasgow when he finds a door across the street. Dwayne is lucky to be alive for one thing because he has a hole in his stomach shaped like an 'M'. He's 26 years old, his beard is as long as two 30cm rulers and he has dark hair as dark as midnight. Dwayne approaches the door and finds... a spacecraft landing on the moon. He goes inside and it's Santa's workshop with a conveyor belt that goes on forever.

Dwayne goes to a window that has a warning saying: 'Don't open the curtains'. So he walks away and puts two presents in his bag and searches even more. He finds a basketball hoop and takes a basketball from the conveyor belt and starts playing.

Dwayne goes back to the window and opens the curtains. He sees Santa's evil spy behind the curtains. The spy stares at him waiting for Dwayne to move.

Dwayne makes a move, running past the trees. He throws a basketball at the spy and he falls over. Dwayne stares at the spy but then the spy gets back up. Dwayne gets to the door just in time!

Dwayne is now home but he can't find the door again. He wants to go back through the door so he opens the two presents. In the two presents are a drone and a VR headset and he decides to give them to his two kids.

Josh Johnston (10)
Woodburn Primary School, Dalkeith

Joe And The Dust Storm

One early morning, Joe was eating his breakfast when he saw something shiny coming from the door. "What's that?" he said. He went to open it but when he opened it it was just a wall. He tried to touch it but his hand went right through the wall and he fell through.

Thud! He landed in a desert then he saw a town so he went to talk to them. "Hi," said Joe.

A villager said, "You are in the Wild West. It's 1880. Are you a cowboy?"

"No," said Joe.

"Anyway, I must warn you not to go in the storm."

"Okay," said Joe so he went to explore the town. First, he went to the clothes shop and bought some clothes. Then he went to the bar and got a drink. But then he forgot what the man said. Finally, he went to the weapons shop to get weapons to kill the dust storm, then he saw the dust storm coming.

Joe ran at the dust storm and swiped at it with his sword but the sword just went right through. Joe fell and got picked up by the storm swirling around in the storm. He spotted the eye of the storm so Joe grabbed it and the storm disappeared. Joe went back to the town and went to his house.

Joe felt like a hero that day but the weird thing was that he never found the portal again.

Harvey Morland (9)
Woodburn Primary School, Dalkeith

Gingerbread Village

I came home from school and went to my fish. I saw a door that I hadn't seen before so I put my bag down and opened it. The door started to suck me in. There was snow but it tasted like icing. There was a gingerbread man. "Hi, I'm Jerri. Are you new here?" Jerri said.

"Yes," I said.

The whole place was made of sweets. There was a rainbow made out of fizzy rainbow belts and the lights were Skittles. I loved it there. I went to the lake. It was frozen. There were little gingerbread boys and girls but I saw this man trying to break the ice. Suddenly, the icy lake broke. I ran down to the icy lake and I helped the children get out. No one knew who I was.

The next day I went to the shops. It was the 30th of November so all the parents were buying Advent calendars. I saw the man again. He was stealing all the calendars! I was chasing him and he fell. I got him to the floor and took his mask off. It was Jerri!

"Why are you doing this to all the children in the gingerbread village?" I said.

"I don't know, I just don't like Christmas," Jerry said.

"I need to go now but I'll be coming back so give all the calendars back, okay?" I said.

"Okay," he said. "Bye."

Amelie McBeth (10)
Woodburn Primary School, Dalkeith

Miniature City

At eight o'clock, I was going to bed. Just as I opened the door leading to my bedroom, I froze. All of a sudden, I felt a strange tingling feeling and the furniture began to grow, or was I shrinking? *Bang!* A tall wooden door appeared. Loudly, the door squeaked open. Shaking nervously, I decided to walk in. On the other side, there was a tall door ten times the size of me and a small crack in the wall. I went through the crack in the wall. As if it were magic, what seemed like an old crack in the wall turned out to be a busy city. The cars were busily driving and noise was everywhere. A small figure loomed in the background.

"Hello, I am Harold the hamster," said the small figure. Harold had chestnut-brown fur and was holding a candy cane. "This place is not safe, we've got to get you home," Harold said, panicking. He tapped his candy cane and we were in a fluffy hallway that was as fluffy as a cloud. The walls were painted pink and white. "Get down on your hands and knees and follow me," said Harold. So I did.

I felt myself start to grow. We came across three doors. "Go through the middle door," exclaimed Harold. He started to fade away. I went through the middle door and I was in my bedroom, safe.

Ava Costello (10)
Woodburn Primary School, Dalkeith

Portal Story

Late on a Monday night, Mia was walking as usual down the streets. She walked past a lonely alleyway and saw a door at the bottom. Of course, she went down to explore! She looked around and found that she was in Candyland. Mia was hoping everything was edible!

Suddenly a lizard came out of behind a rock and said to Mia, "Don't stay here for more than twenty-four hours," then the lizard ran off.

Mia thought it was quite strange. Mia looked at her watch and saw the time. She had only ten minutes to get out. She rushed to find the door to get back. She heard a voice behind her and she turned around to see the king staring and laughing at her. She asked what was wrong and he said, "You're not going anywhere!"

Mia ran and ran. She got to a canyon. She said to herself, "I am not gonna make it, the king is getting closer." She saw a gem behind a rock and it had a note saying: 'Use this when you need to get back to your own world. All you have to do is rub it twice and it should teleport you back to your original world'.

Mia quickly picked it up and rubbed it twice. Mia was successful and made it back to her own world. She realised she still had the gem. She was so amazed. Mia continued her peaceful walk.

Amber Brown (10)
Woodburn Primary School, Dalkeith

The Magic Door

Zack was a short boy with a small head. He also had a bendy neck, tiny fingers, scary eyes, double swords, stinky socks, short hair and a mask. He loved going to new places and buying new stuff. The Halloween workshop was where scary ghosts, zombies, pumpkin heads and some small baby bats were 'so scary'. The workshop sold costumes like zombie costumes, skeleton costumes, werewolf costumes and more.

Zack was warned not to be scared or run away from the workshop and not to kill. If he killed anything he would be eaten by the zombies. So he tried not to do anything like killing.

He knocked on the door and obviously got scared by the bat and killed one of them then ran away. He ran because he remembered the rules in the workshop: 'If you run away or kill any of the scary monsters you will die'... So he was really, really scared! And behind the door was a ghost.

He ran as fast as he could to the portal because he'd disobeyed the rules of the workshop.

He escaped out from the portal and the portal disappeared just after he left but he realised that there was something that escaped with him too. It was a magical item. The magical item was a magical sword which was double, his favourite combination.

Tolu Oloni (10)
Woodburn Primary School, Dalkeith

Fortnite Door

Hi, my name is Oliver and I like to play a game called Fortnite.

One morning, I was out for a walk with my granny's dog. At the bottom of the hill there was a door that was wide open. I thought that I was imagining things but at that moment I heard a gunshot. Suddenly the door disappeared... So I carried on walking but then I thought to myself that it looked like a game called Fortnite but the glitch version. Suddenly the door appeared again. I suddenly walked through the door and saw the Fortnite island but it was a glitch.

I saw the battle bus on the island that I was on. I think it was the spawn island so I ran over to the battle bus and jumped on at the last second. The battle bus was going so fast it was faster than a rocket ship. I thought to myself, *I will jump out of the battle bus at the big tower at the end.* In order to jump I needed a parachute and I saw one. I grabbed it and jumped out of the battle bus. I slowly began to fly. I looked at where I was going to land and sky-dived down to the place.

I landed on a building and I began to loot. I got a gun and shot a car and it blew up. I thought to myself, *I will stay here*. And then I walked off and I never saw door the door again.

Oliver Lovatt (10)
Woodburn Primary School, Dalkeith

The Forest Space Adventure

I was sitting in my room one day when I decided to take my dog on a walk to the forest. It was a pretty normal walk at first until we saw a door. I asked my dog, that was magic, what it was. He said that it was a magic door and it would take us to space! So I opened the door and we got sucked away!

While we were being shot up to space we got spacesuits put on us. And before we knew it we could see the whole solar system. The sun, Mercury, Venus, Earth, Mars, Jupiter, Saturn, Neptune and Uranus, and also the two asteroid belts. It was beautiful! Then something crazy happened... There was an asteroid going to the door we came from. But luckily it was a near miss. We could see amazing, shining stars. But we couldn't look at it for long because it was so bright it could blind us. But guess what happened?

We met an alien! His name was Alfie the alien. He was 4.6 billion years old because aliens live forever.

He couldn't understand me so we used sign language. He said that we had to get out of there because the universe was going to have the big bang again. So we floated as fast as we could to the magic door and the big bang pushed us so hard we went through the door and landed back in the forest!

Lyall Evans-Thomson (10)
Woodburn Primary School, Dalkeith

The Wonders Of Space

A doorway suddenly appeared, towering high above me. It seems like it was made for a giant because it was huge. The door was covered with stars, suns and planets which was beautiful and amazing. But I couldn't reach the door handle. I noticed some big boxes behind a bush. I managed to pick them up and I put them in front of the door like a staircase. I opened the door and a flash of light blinded me.

What I saw was remarkable. It was the cosmos, stars, sun, planets, gas giant planets and galaxies. But then I saw a demonic, inhuman spaceship. It had an alien pilot. The spaceship came right up to me and I thought it was going to abduct me and I would never see my family again. However, it was actually friendly and helped me out by opening the door for me and saying goodbye. I said, "Goodbye," and then I went out the door. But something wasn't right so I went back through the door and quickly realised the alien and its spaceship was in trouble. It had landed on an unknown planet, so I tried to help it out.

I managed to get off the planet and then I said my last goodbyes. I went through the door, arrived home and then I cooked porridge for my family.

Jack Fryatt (10)
Woodburn Primary School, Dalkeith

My Secret Time In New York

One day, a black door appeared in my room. I heard barking and all sorts of animal noises. I was really excited because I thought Mum got me a new puppy but it turned out she hadn't. I knocked on the door as treats fell out but that dragged me to go in even more.

After a couple of minutes of lying down on my bed, I decided to go in. I couldn't believe my eyes, there was a pet shop behind that door. A girl stepped out from behind the counter and froze.

I moved around the shop, checking no one else was in there. Then I started to realise that everything started to grow, or was I shrinking? What was going to happen? I was so scared and all of a sudden I screamed.

Looking out of the window I saw a shining light and a lot of people. Where could I be? I was in the United States of America and it took 20 minutes to get from my bedroom to there. Oh my goodness, I was in NYC! I saw the Empire State Building, Macy's, Central Park and the Christmas tree.

Checking no one was looking I ran like an idiot. I went to all the shops that I have ever wanted to go to. Then I got nauseous and fell on the ground and woke up in my room. It was all a dream!

Lucy McCluskey (10)
Woodburn Primary School, Dalkeith

Winter Wonderland

Lauren is a kind girl. She is fifteen years old. She was going to a party, but on the way she saw a mysterious door with lovely-looking leaves on it. She slowly and carefully stepped inside.

In front of her, there was a wonderful winter world where the snow never stopped falling. There were candy canes and snowmen. She was having so much fun. There was even Santa's grotto and Rudolph was there.

Suddenly a boy dressed in a bright red suit with a heavy red crown on his head appeared. His name was Fire Boy. He told Lauren to never ever touch the pink candy cane or something terrible would happen.

Lauren got hungry and tried to eat the pink candy cane but the candy cane opened and a button appeared. Lauren hit it.

She got teleported into an underground lair. Everything was bright red and Fire Boy was standing there. He said, "What did I tell you?" Lauren ran for miles and miles and finally, she found the door.

Lauren got out but the door disappeared, she thought she was dreaming but when she got home she found in her bag a snow globe with a replica of the winter wonderland inside.

Becca Yeoman (10)

Woodburn Primary School, Dalkeith

Santa's Magical Workshop

Georgie was slowly walking to the shops when she saw a door with candy canes painted on it. She walked towards it then held the handle and twisted it.

She was amazed to find Santa's workshop. Georgie saw a figure standing outside the workshop so she strolled towards it. She introduced herself as Lucy. Lucy had long ginger hair and emerald-green eyes. She told Georgie she should pull a candy cane out of the ground. Georgie didn't know if it was a good idea but Lucy sounded persuasive so Georgie said she'd do it.

There was a sleigh with loads of presents with red and green fairy lights. Presents glimmered and glowed on top of the tables. Lollipops and candy canes made her mouth water.

Georgie heard a whisper in her ear... "Pull the candy cane out of the ground." With no hesitation, Georgie stepped towards a candy cane and pulled it out of the ground.

When Georgie turned to leave, Lucy was gone and the door was disappearing. She ran so fast, still holding onto the candy cane, Georgie made it back to normal land. The candy cane began to spark, maybe it was magical...

Avah Marshall (10)
Woodburn Primary School, Dalkeith

Sunny's Adventure

One day a girl called Sunny was having a morning stroll in the woods. Sunny had ocean-like eyes, she also had lovely long blonde hair and was very kind. She suddenly saw a door. It had a pawprint on it and a wing marking. Sunny cautiously approached the door and tried to open it but it wouldn't budge. She finally fell through the door and a lion came up to her and said, "Hello, my name is Ember, never cross the river!"

That night Sunny went across to see why the animals were so scared. Bulldozers and tree choppers were destroying the land. Sunny decided to go back and help the animals fight. They tripped over all the animals. The only person standing was the evil person that was in the bulldozer. Sunny found some rope on the floor and wrapped it around her. The animals put her in the animal dungeon and one of the animals said the door was closing. Sunny raced to the door and the animals gave her a hug. The animals said, "You may come back once a year."

Sunny went through the portal. She reached into her pocket. A rock was in it and it said 'thank you'.

Amber Marshall (10)
Woodburn Primary School, Dalkeith

The Ice-Breaking Curse

One cold, frosty day, I was looking at the ice on the pavement. When I was at school that's when I saw something grow out of the ice. An ice door appeared in front of me and I said, "Guys, look at this!"

They said, "Look at what?"

They thought I was playing a joke but when I looked away it started to crack. As quickly as I could I took a massive breath and opened the door. My friends behind me watched till they saw me disappear. When they saw me vanish into thin air they screamed until all the attention was on them. While they told everyone the story I was on cold ice. I looked down and saw a polar bear trapped under the water. As I could hardly think I realised I had ice skates on. As quickly as I could take a breath I took my skates off and stabbed the blade into the ice, setting the polar bear free. I saw an ice-cold island to direct the polar bear to. He showed me a door then it opened. It took me to my classroom. My friends stared at me and said, "Where were you?"

That was the day I met a polar bear.

Kaitlyn Clark (10)
Woodburn Primary School, Dalkeith

The Magic Door

One day, Tim was visiting the Empire State Building, investigating the basement. Using his phone flashlight he saw a red door with magical stars flashing and swirling around it. Tim had a growth mindset and was super brave. He tiptoed to the door and opened it as slowly as a turtle. Through the doorway, he saw raining lava and a giant volcano far away. Tim was scared of the explosion and bangs and the lava was hissing like a snake. Shaking and sweating, he was full of scaredness. Tim fell over a hot rock and heard a crack on his arm.

"Ow!" shouted Tim, his arm was broken. Tim took his water gun out of his bag and fired at the lava. The lava hissed as it cooled down, turning into obsidian. Tim fired his water gun at the volcano and all the lava cooled down. Then he packed up and went back to the door, he slammed the door shut then he was back in the Empire State Building's basement.

Tim's twin, Tom, took him to the hospital to get a cast on his arm. Tom thought he didn't believe his brother's story.

Kearyn Adamson (10)
Woodburn Primary School, Dalkeith

The Abandoned Hotel

One day there was a boy that loved swimming and had black hair, called Robert, he was going to the cinema. He saw a strange-looking door so he went to the door and slowly opened it.

When Robert got in he saw a very scary-looking hotel and saw that it was about to rain, thunder and lightning so he went inside the hotel and strangely saw a lot of doors. He said, "This is very creepy." Robert saw a boy and said, "Hi, what is your name?"

The boy said that he'd seen a man that had red hair and had evil creations. He also stole an orb from someone.

Robert saw an elevator so he went in. He went all the way to the final floor and saw the scary and evil man with the strange orb. So he stole the orb as fast as he could.

The man started chasing Robert. Robert saw a vent so he went in the vent. Thankfully the man didn't fit in the vent so Robert was safe.

Robert rubbed the orb three times and it teleported him to the cinema. So he watched a movie and enjoyed it a lot.

Ibrahim Mohammed (9)
Woodburn Primary School, Dalkeith

The Trip To Space

I walked through the magic door and I was at NASA, about to travel on my ship to the International Space Station. I got there, said bye to everyone and took off. I saw a black hole and it was a very big one. It was black, and massive with stars everywhere. I finally got to the International Space Station. I went to fix a part of it which was the United Kingdom's part.

A meteor flew past me fast. I told everyone there and we had to radio back to NASA. I came back and got supplies for the international crew. I got back on my ship and flew up to the International Space Station. Excitedly, I saw another black hole. I got there and put the supplies away.

The next day, I woke up in surprise because everyone was singing happy birthday to me. It was my birthday. I was so happy, I went home, had something to eat and said bye to the black hole. When I got there I had steak, gravy and vegetables and went out to party. By the way, the names of the crew were Macy, George, me and Bob.

James Halliday (10)
Woodburn Primary School, Dalkeith

The Magic Door

Hi, my name is Lilly. I have blonde hair and I am short. One afternoon I was walking home from school and I saw a mysterious door. It had fairy lights and stockings, even candy canes and tiny Christmas trees. I saw it when I came out of school early. So I went and opened the door and went in. The magic door led me to a winter wonderland. It was out of this world. It even had a ginormous candy cane but it had a North Pole sign saying *The North Pole Is This Way*.

When I was walking through it I saw a man saying, "Don't eat the candy canes," so I started to walk again then I saw a field of candy canes. I couldn't resist eating one and then I ate about ten or twenty more candy canes and I then I felt sick. But suddenly I saw the monster again that was holding the sign. He was screaming at me like a pterodactyl. Then I found a cherry-flavoured cane that took me home. When I got home I said, "Finally, I'm home."

Phoebe Bees (10)
Woodburn Primary School, Dalkeith

Winter Wonderland

One day Alex was walking home from school when he saw a mysterious door.

Alex opened it and saw a winter wonderland with candy corn, snow and candy canes. He said, "I need to try every goody, sweet, tasty treat here!" Alex loved it but then a thing appeared above his head that said: 'Warning - do not speak to the white rabbit'.

Alex was sure he was not going to speak to the white rabbit but he was wrong. Alex wanted to go to a candy store! But little did he know he was in for a treat. He ordered candy corn, candy canes and way more but then he saw the white rabbit. He realised he was speaking to the rabbit. Then a warning symbol appeared above his head that said: 'You must leave in the next two minutes or you will not exist in the real world'.

So he ran twice as fast as a cheetah so he could catch the magic door before it disappeared. He got there just in time and he took 100 magical crystals home to safety.

Ellie Wright (10)
Woodburn Primary School, Dalkeith

The Bear Island

One day a little boy named Colin saw a door so he went through the door. He felt dizzy then he was on an island. He saw a village and a boy called Denis. He said, "Let's go hunt."

"But I do not kill animals."

But he said, "I will do all the work."

So Colin said, "Okay."

In a large field, they sat for hours then Colin ran away. Denis tried to kick Colin so they were fighting but Colin won the fight. Denis did not give up so Colin used karate on him. He was crying and went to his mom then Colin was fighting lots of people. He won the big fight but they kicked him out of the village. Then he saw a house then a lion came to him. I ran away then a king with a sword tried to kill him so he was panicking. He was a fierce king and he had a long beard. His name was Jake. Then the portal came back for Colin then he was taken back. He saw his mum and ran to her happily.

Kai Keogh (9)
Woodburn Primary School, Dalkeith

Santa Claus

Last night, I was going to bed but the door was very different. I thought my mum and dad changed it because I had been out all day with my friends but with two breaths I walked in... *Boom!*

Was I Santa Claus? Was I about to leave the North Pole...? Well, I guess I'm Santa for the night. On the other hand, do I really want to be Santa? I mean, yes but no! The door was right there. "Let's go with my gut, yes," I chose. "*Elfff!*" I shouted. "What do I do?"

"You know what to do, Santa."

Oh my gosh, I didn't even tell him.

12 hours later... "This is my last stop. Dalkeith, here we go. This is my house. Bye, Santa's sleigh. Finally, I've finished. I'm literally so tired. After 13 hours of hard work. I've made it. Home sweet home. I'm so happy, I'm never going through that weird door again."

Arran Singh (10)
Woodburn Primary School, Dalkeith

Under The Sea

I was in school and I was bored and asked to go to the toilet. I was in the toilet and suddenly there was a door that was as blue as the sky and as wet as the sea. Soggy seaweed was on top of the door. Opening the door I jumped in and I was under the sea!

I could feel the seaweed tickling my feet as I swam through the deep darkness. There was a shipwreck with treasure everywhere. I grabbed as much as I could then I heard a loud roar. I felt petrified. It was as loud as a plane.

I started to swim for my life and luckily, I found an underwater city and took a rest. Then I heard the roar but even louder this time, which meant it was creeping closer but I couldn't swim away. It was right in front of me so I just stayed as still as a statue.

Later, I saw the door so I swam to it as fast as I could and I escaped.

Jamie Moffat (10)
Woodburn Primary School, Dalkeith

The Day I Fell Into A Rainforest

One scorching day, I was working at the zoo and I needed to feed the snakes. But the door looked different. It had vines, leaves, and a snake looking through the keyhole. With no hesitation, I opened the door. And before I knew it I was falling into a bush. I wasn't in the snake enclosure, I was in the rainforest!

I started exploring. I saw waterfalls, vines, leaves and animals. But one second later I was in danger. I was exploring and I saw two massive alligators. They had green humps on their backs. They were walking toward me. Then they finally waddled away, I was relieved. I felt like I was in Jumanji. Then before I knew it it was raining so I looked for shelter. I was over the moon when I saw a cave. But there was a door at the end of the cave... With no hesitation, I opened it...

Arran Campbell (10)
Woodburn Primary School, Dalkeith

Portal Story

One sunny day Nathan goes to the post office as he usually does but there is something unusual, there is a door. Just an ordinary door...

He walks over to the door and jumps in. This place is half cold, half hot and there are glaciers on the cold side. There is a creature called Dynama that will eat anything living and there are dead body berries. Then Nathan eats some berries.

A guy called Will walks over to him and tells him not to spend thirty minutes on either side. Nathan falls asleep on the hot side and disobeys the warning then he wakes up. Then he sees Dynama. Dynama sees him and starts rushing towards him. Will starts sprinting for the door and dives in. He manages to get out as the door slams. He never finds the door again.

Kaleb Watson (10)
Woodburn Primary School, Dalkeith

Haunted Hotel

One day ago, James went to the shops wearing a red jumper. After the shops, he went to his house and he found a door in his back garden. He opened the door and went in. The door took him to a haunted hotel. It had smashed-up windows, torn-up floorboards and ripped-up couches but there was a note on the wall. It said: 'Don't stay in the same room for more than one hour'.

James broke rule one trying to find the key and then he found the key but he realised he had been in the room for more than one hour! He ran!

He couldn't find the door but then he found a wand and waved it about. The wand transported him back to his garden. He warned everyone never to go through the door again.

Lewis Thomson (9)
Woodburn Primary School, Dalkeith

True Culinary Experience

Hi, today I found something beautiful. Well, I was walking in the woods when I found a door. Then I went inside. I walked in and saw a kitchen flooded with people and food. I didn't want to stay so I turned to go back but there only was a freezer. Suddenly the kitchen fell silent. I looked around and saw a chef with a crown on his hat. "Why is there so much shouting?"
You would think I'm sensitive to noise. Because I am! I turned back around and surprise, surprise, the door was back! So I went through it.

Harley Dean (10)
Woodburn Primary School, Dalkeith

The Jungle

I saw this magic door. I opened the door and there was a jungle. I saw a monkey. In the jungle, there were lots of trees. I saw a tiger, he was running towards me. I jumped on his back. He was running really fast. There were snakes, the snakes were following me. I was running really fast. I jumped on a tree. The snakes went away. I was safe. *How am I going to get back to the door?* I thought.
I saw the tiger again. I jumped on his back and he took me to the door. I went in the door. What a crazy day!

Harrison Gifford (10)
Woodburn Primary School, Dalkeith

The World Cup

One day I found a magic door. It was covered with footballs and the flag of Qatar. I entered it and I was surrounded by people. We were cheering, and dancing. Suddenly the magic door came and I jumped in the door and I found myself in my bed. Then the door came again, this time it took me to a match. The match was Qatar vs Ecuador. The scores were 2-0. I thought that France would win because their team had very good players.
The portal took me back to my bed and I slept.

Praise Mhango (10)
Woodburn Primary School, Dalkeith

YoungWriters®
— Est. 1991 —

Young Writers Information

We hope you have enjoyed reading this book – and that you will continue to in the coming years.

If you're the parent or family member of an enthusiastic poet or story writer, do visit our website **www.youngwriters.co.uk/subscribe** and sign up to receive news, competitions, writing challenges and tips, activities and much, much more! There's lots to keep budding writers motivated!

If you would like to order further copies of this book, or any of our other titles, then please give us a call or order via your online account.

Young Writers
Remus House
Coltsfoot Drive
Peterborough
PE2 9BF
(01733) 890066
info@youngwriters.co.uk

Join in the conversation!
Tips, news, giveaways and much more!

 **YoungWritersUK**  **YoungWritersCW** 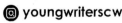 **youngwriterscw**